Y0-CDJ-710

# Joe Louis

These and other titles are included in The Importance Of biography series:

Alexander the Great
Muhammad Ali
Louis Armstrong
James Baldwin
Clara Barton
Charlemagne
Napoleon Bonaparte
Julius Caesar
Rachel Carson
Charlie Chaplin
Cesar Chavez
Winston Churchill
Cleopatra
Christopher Columbus
Hernando Cortes
Marie Curie
Amelia Earhart
Thomas Edison
Albert Einstein
Duke Ellington
Dian Fossey
Benjamin Franklin
Galileo Galilei
Emma Goldman
Jane Goodall
Martha Graham
Stephen Hawking
Jim Henson
Adolf Hitler
Harry Houdini
Thomas Jefferson
Mother Jones
Chief Joseph
Joe Louis
Malcolm X
Margaret Mead
Michelangelo
Wolfgang Amadeus Mozart
John Muir
Sir Isaac Newton
Richard M. Nixon
Georgia O'Keeffe
Louis Pasteur
Pablo Picasso
Elvis Presley
Jackie Robinson
Norman Rockwell
Anwar Sadat
Margaret Sanger
Oskar Schindler
John Steinbeck
Tecumseh
Jim Thorpe
Thurgood Marshall
Mark Twain
Queen Victoria
Pancho Villa
H. G. Wells

*To Brenda Campbell and Candice Busch, who are fighting their own battles with all the courage and determination of true champions*

THE IMPORTANCE OF

# Joe Louis

by
Jim Campbell

Lucent Books, P.O. Box 289011, San Diego, CA 92198-9011

Library of Congress Cataloging-in-Publication Data

Campbell, Jim, 1937–
Joe Louis / by Jim Campbell.
p. cm.—(The importance of)
Includes bibliographical references (p. ) and index.
Summary: Discusses the life of the heavyweight boxing champion who became a symbol of success and determination not just for blacks but for all Americans.
ISBN 1-56006-085-9 (alk. paper)
1. Louis, Joe, 1914–1981 —Juvenile literature. 2. Afro-American boxers—Biography—Juvenile literature. [1. Louis, Joe, 1914–1981 2. Boxers (Sports) 3. Afro-American—Biography.] I. Title. II. Series.
GV1132.L6C36 1997
796.8'3'092—dc21 96–47849
[B] CIP
AC



Printed in the U.S.A.

# Contents

# Foreword

THE IMPORTANCE OF biography series deals with individuals who have made a unique contribution to history. The editors of the series have deliberately chosen to cast a wide net and include people from all fields of endeavor. Individuals from politics, music, art, literature, philosophy, science, sports, and religion are all represented. In addition, the editors did not restrict the series to individuals whose accomplishments have helped change the course of history. Of necessity, this criterion would have eliminated many whose contribution was great, though limited. Charles Darwin, for example, was responsible for radically altering the scientific view of the natural history of the world. His achievements continue to impact the study of science today. Others, such as Chief Joseph of the Nez Percé, played a pivotal role in the history of their own people. While Joseph's influence does not extend much beyond the Nez Percé, his nonviolent resistance to white expansion and his continuing role in protecting his tribe and his homeland remain an inspiration to all.

These biographies are more than factual chronicles. Each volume attempts to emphasize an individual's contributions both in his or her own time and for posterity. For example, the voyages of Christopher Columbus opened the way to European colonization of the New World. Unquestionably, his encounter with the New World brought monumental changes to both Europe and the Americas in his day. Today, however, the broader impact of Columbus's voyages is being critically scrutinized. *Christopher Columbus,* as well as every biography in The Importance Of series, includes and evaluates the most recent scholarship available on each subject.

Each author includes a wide variety of primary and secondary source quotations to document and substantiate his or her work. All quotes are footnoted to show readers exactly how and where biographers derive their information, as well as provide stepping stones to further research. These quotations enliven the text by giving readers eyewitness views of the life and times of each individual covered in The Importance Of series.

Finally, each volume is enhanced by photographs, bibliographies, chronologies, and comprehensive indexes. For both the casual reader and the student engaged in research, The Importance Of biographies will be a fascinating adventure into the lives of people who have helped shape humanity's past and present, and who will continue to shape its future.

## Important Dates in the Life of Joe Louis

**1914**
Joe Louis Barrow is born in Chambers County, Alabama, on May 13.

**1926**
Mother remarries; moves with family to Detroit.

**1932**
Begins training in a Detroit gym and enters Golden Gloves competition.

**1934**
Turns professional and comes under the tutelage of managers John Roxborough and Julian Black and trainer Jack "Chappie" Blackburn. First pro bout is a first-round knockout over Jack Kracken—Louis earns fifty-two dollars.

**1935**
Fights Primo Carnera—the first of several former heavyweight champions he will meet and defeat—in New York on June 25. Louis wins with sixth-round knockout.

**1936**
Hits lowest point in career as shocking loss to Max Schmeling derails drive to championship.

**1937**
Wins heavyweight championship of the world by knocking out Jim Braddock in Chicago on June 22.

**1938**
Vindicates himself by knocking out Schmeling in two minutes, four seconds in the first round of the rematch.

**1939**
Begins defending title against all comers; risks his title twenty-five times in his career.

**1942**
Donates two purses from championship bouts to Navy Relief and Army Relief as United States goes to war.

**1945**
After serving forty-six months in U.S. Army, returns to civilian life.

**1946**
Defends title for the first time in four years against Billy Conn; wins by a knockout in the eighth.

**1949**
Announces retirement as undefeated heavyweight champion of the world on March 1, but does not quit.

**1951**
Loses the title to Rocky Marciano and retires for good.

**1977**
Suffers disabling stroke and is confined to wheelchair the rest of his life.

**1981**
Dies in Las Vegas on April 12 and is buried with full military honors at Arlington National Cemetery.

**1993**
U.S. Postal Service honors Louis with a commemorative postage stamp.

# A Role Model

By 1945 Joe Louis had became a symbol of success and determination not just for blacks but for all Americans, regardless of race, creed, color, or national origin. When he defeated German boxer Max Schmeling in a dramatic, first-round knockout in 1938, almost everyone accepted the sensational boxer as simply an "American."

At the time Louis began boxing in 1932, the sport was second only to major

*Joe Louis (right) hammers away at opponent Lou Nova during a 1941 fight. Louis is remembered as perhaps the greatest boxer of all time.*

league baseball as the sport most followed by the public. Therefore, a well-known boxer was a celebrated citizen. Because baseball is a team game, and boxing an individual sport, some historians argue that the champion of boxing's most important division, heavyweight, is the most important sports figure of his time. Louis, certainly, would go on to fit this description.

When Joe Louis won the title of world champion heavyweight boxer in 1937, he was on his way toward becoming the most recognized sports figure in the world. He achieved this level of fame when television did not exist and radio was relatively new. People heard about Louis through newspapers, magazines, and movie newsreels.

Born in poverty in the rural, strictly segregated South in 1914, Louis, like many other southern blacks, moved to the industrial North as a youngster. He first became interested in boxing at the age of seventeen while living in Detroit. Louis used money that his mother gave him for violin lessons to pay the locker rental fee at a local gym.

## No Jack Johnson

When Louis turned professional in 1934, he had a heavy burden on his shoulders. As a black boxer, he had to live down the legacy of Jack Johnson. Johnson, the heavyweight champion from 1908 to 1915, was perceived by the vast majority of whites—many of them prejudiced against blacks—as an arrogant and undesirable person who did not deserve the title of heavyweight boxing champion of the world. The influence of the white majority, who dictated what was acceptable in the country at the time, prevented black boxers from fighting for the heavyweight championship from the time Jackson lost it (1915) until Louis won it in 1937. Louis's conduct had to be beyond reproach and criticism from the white community if he was to succeed.

## Rules to Live By

When Louis rose through the ranks of amateur boxing and was about to become a professional prizefighter, his managers laid down certain rules for him so he would be as different from Jack Johnson as possible. Louis followed the advice of his handlers and was accepted by the general public while becoming a symbol of hope to his race.

In the 1930s few black men, and practically no black women, had much fame or celebrity. Entertainers Bill "Bojangles" Robinson, Louis "Satchmo" Armstrong, and Paul Robeson, as well as athlete Jesse Owens, were among the few blacks to achieve some degree of fame. A significant portion of the nation's newspapers did not cover black achievements on a regular basis. Joe Louis changed all that.

## The Nation's Hope

Joe Louis, through hard work and determination, made himself a great boxer. Louis was far from a natural athlete. He was big and strong, but any quickness he achieved came through long and repetitious workouts and practice sessions. The effort paid off in the end. Early accounts

*In a country deeply divided along racial lines, Joe Louis was a powerful force in the fight for civil rights.*

of his fights talk about his lightning speed, his fancy footwork, and his quick reflexes. Louis became what is still regarded by many today as the ultimate fighting machine.

When Louis became heavyweight champion of the world, he was able to influence those in power to provide a better life and more equal treatment for his people and other minorities. While Louis was a soldier in the U.S. Army during World War II, for example, he was able to arrange for a significant number of qualified blacks to be accepted to officer candidate school. He was even instrumental in getting Jackie Robinson, the man who broke major league baseball's modern color line, to play on the Fort Riley baseball team, when both were stationed at the famous cavalry post in Kansas during World War II.

Long after Louis's final retirement in 1951, he remained an American hero, a legend. He is still regarded as one of the greatest, if not the greatest, boxers of all time.

Chapter

# 1 Down Yonder

Nothing in Joe Louis's early life would indicate future greatness. Joe Louis Barrow was born the seventh of eight children in the red clay country of Chambers County, Alabama, on May 13, 1914. His sharecropper parents, Munroe "Mun" Barrow and Lillie Reese Barrow, fought hard and unyielding soil to raise mostly cotton.

Joe's early childhood was marked by his father's illness. When Joe was two, his father was committed to the epileptic ward of the Searcy State Hospital for the Colored Insane at Mt. Vernon, Alabama. It is unclear whether Munroe Barrow was truly epileptic or suffered from mental illness: At the time, people who suffered from epilepsy were treated as though they were mentally unstable.

Oddly enough, his father remained a presence in Louis's life, as he would often escape from the hospital and visit his family, once staying two years.

## Southern Roots

When the family received word that Joe's father had died in the hospital, his mother single-handedly reared her eight children and worked the land. She was proud of her ability to do a man's work—plowing the fields, planting and picking cotton, and cutting wood by the cord like a lumberjack. She later married a man named

*Joe Louis's father, Munroe Barrow, pictured with four of Joe's brothers and sisters. After Munroe's death, Louis's mother single-handedly reared her eight children in the rural South.*

*Factories like the Ford Motor Company (pictured) lured workers to the industrial cities of the North. Like so many others of this era, Joe's family migrated to Detroit in search of factory work.*

Pat Brooks, who had five children of his own. Joe said, "He [Brooks] gave us Barrows a break. He was a good stepfather. He was the only father I ever knew."[1]

Shortly after Brooks became Joe's stepfather, the family moved to another piece of land, farther back in the Buckalew Mountains near the town of Mt. Sinai. Joe remembered the new life as another hardscrabble existence. "We didn't wear shoes much and we kept our good clothes for Sundays. We had only kerosene lamps in the shack, it was pretty grim."[2]

Years later a reporter asked him about his youth, saying, "Joe, when you were a kid, did you ever dream to be a champion and a millionaire?"

Louis replied, "I couldn't dream that big."[3]

Joe not only gained a stepfather when his mother remarried, he gained a best friend in his stepbrother Pat, who was about Joe's age. The boys did their chores and played games together. One of the things Joe remembered best was how he and Pat were allowed to ride in the mule-drawn wagon on the soft and bouncy cotton on the way to the cotton gin in town.

Joe attended school at Mt. Sinai Baptist Church. Attendance was not very strictly enforced, and the school was in session only from October until April when school-age children were not needed to work the land and to do other jobs.

Joe often played hooky to wander the nearby woods and fields. When he did go to school, his stuttering made him an object of ridicule.

## Move to the Motor City

In 1926, when Joe was about twelve years old, some Brooks relatives who had moved north several years earlier returned to Alabama for a vacation. They talked about the plentiful, well-paid jobs in Detroit, the Motor City, and how the automobile manufacturers, especially Ford Motor Company, would hire blacks as well as whites. These factories were the product of industrialist Henry Ford, who invented the assembly line and needed workers to mass produce his famous Model T.

Thousands of people—black and white—were migrating to the larger industrial cities of the North to work in the many mills and factories that were producing the goods and products people demanded.

Throughout the late 1920s, many American families were enjoying prosperity as a result of the great economic growth the nation experienced after World War I. Work was plentiful. Wages were at an all-time high, and people had what became known as disposable income.

Pat Brooks went north first and later sent for his large family. At first the Barrow-Brooks clan lived with relatives, but they soon rented a small apartment in a tenement on Catherine Street on Detroit's East Side.

## School Days

Joe enrolled in the third grade at Duffield Elementary School. Duffield's routine of different classrooms, assemblies, fire drills, and many different teachers was hard for Joe to adjust to, yet his teachers liked the big, quiet boy from the South. They allowed him to carry the American flag at assemblies, as he would later carry the hope of America into the boxing ring. Joe later described that honor:

> That was supposed to be some kind of honor job. No way could I mess that up. I was tall, strong, and they tell me, I was a nice-looking kid. Those assembly days, Momma made sure I had a clean, starched white shirt and blue necktie. That's the only thing about school that I really liked.[4]

Joe and his friend and classmate Freddie Guinyard attended Calvary Baptist Church together. They would also visit the Eastern Market near their Detroit neighborhood to look for jobs moving crates of produce on market days. With Freddie's outgoing, talkative nature and Joe's size, they soon had quite a bit of work.

## The Stock Market Crash

While Joe's family was rejoicing at their successful move to Detroit, the stock market crashed in October 1929. Stock prices fell to new lows, businesses were forced to close, fortunes were lost, and large numbers of workers lost their jobs. The depression years that followed the crash were bleak. The nation's banking system collapsed in 1933, causing many of those who had not lost heavily before to lose what they still had. Nearly one worker in four was unemployed. Those who still had jobs earned about 40 percent of what they had earned before.

Joe said later, "Funny thing, I'll bet you can predict a depression just by seeing how many black people are starting to lose their jobs. For the first time, I remember being hungry."[5]

Joe reached the sixth grade, but couldn't seem to get much higher at Duffield School. Miss Vada Schwader, remembered by Joe as "a nice teacher," suggested he try a vocational school. He enrolled at Bronson Vocational, an all-boys school, where he proved to be good with his hands—something a lot of boxers would learn the hard way in the future. He built tables, cabinets, and bookshelves at Bronson, which he took home for his family to use.

When Pat Brooks lost his job, Joe's parents relied on relief and welfare agencies that assisted the unemployed. The family received several hundred dollars during that time. His parents considered the money a loan, intending to repay it when the family's circumstances improved. Joe inherited the debt, eventually repaying it with the money he earned from boxing.

To help during these hard times, Joe and Freddie worked on an ice wagon. Their job was to deliver the huge blocks of ice (usually fifty or one hundred pounds) to their customers every few days to keep food from spoiling. The horse-drawn ice wagons stopped at nearly every house and apartment building in a neighborhood. Wrapping the ice in heavy burlap bags kept it from melting too fast in the warm weather. The smaller Freddie waited with the horses while Joe lugged the heavy blocks of ice up several flights of apartment house steps.

After working long hours at either the Eastern Market or on the ice wagon, Joe looked for entertainment. For five cents, he could spend the evening at the movies. Joe saw his first movies at the Catherine Theatre in Detroit. Like nearly all youngsters of the 1930s, Joe liked the Westerns best, and his heroes were the cowboys Buck Jones, Ken Maynard, and the most famous of them all, Tom Mix.

## Fiddler or Fighter?

Out of the family's meager income, Joe's mother scraped together fifty cents for weekly violin lessons for her son. One day, while Joe was walking to his violin lesson, he met up with his friend Thurston McKinney. McKinney persuaded Joe to skip his lesson and go with him to Brewster's East Side Gymnasium. Joe liked the gym on his first visit. He put on boxing gloves and began working out on the punching bags and other equipment. Joe eventually sparred with McKinney and nearly knocked out the more experienced boxer.

*Unemployed workers sit idle in the streets during the bleak depression era, when nearly one worker in four was unemployed. Louis recalls of this period, "For the first time, I remember being hungry."*

Without telling his mother, Joe used the weekly violin lesson money to pay for his locker at Brewster's gym. He continued to take boxing instruction and to train and eventually entered the local Golden Gloves competition as an amateur novice, or beginner, in late 1932.

## His First Fight

Joe fought his first fight at Detroit's Edison Athletic Club, one of many boxing clubs that were common across the country before television became a popular way of bringing prizefights to boxing fans. Louis remembered the fight this way:

> I weighed about 168 then, and they stacked me against Johnny Miler, a white boy. He had been a fighter for a few years and I was new at it. He had fought in the 1932 Olympics in Los Angeles. I never got a solid punch in against him. He knocked me down seven times in two rounds, more than anyone ever did after that. He mussed me up pretty bad. Going home that night I was sore all over and pretty low. I got a $7 merchandise check out of the fight, that was the loser's share. I gave it to my mother.
>
> She stuck up for me. She told me, "Joe, if you want to keep boxing, you keep with it." She said, "If that's what you want to work at, I'll work for you to get it."[6]

Joe's stepfather wasn't so sure and wanted the boy to get factory work at the Ford plant, which Joe succeeded in doing. But Joe couldn't forget about boxing. Years later, Joe would recall:

*Louis with his mother, Lillie Brooks, who encouraged her son in his athletic endeavors.*

*Joe Louis poses during his early years as a boxer. Louis's incredible dedication and determination made his legendary rise to fame possible.*

> I stayed away from the ring for about six or seven months after I lost that fight. Then I put in for a Golden Gloves tournament. I'm still "on leave" from "B" building. I later saw Henry Ford II and reminded him that I never quit at Ford's. My work card is still there.[7]

Louis's first trainer was a successful black middleweight boxer named Holman Williams. Between his own fights and training sessions, Williams worked with Louis on the basics of boxing. After several weeks of resumed training Williams decided that Louis was ready for another fight. To prepare the fighter for his next match, Williams had Louis spar with a quick, little bantamweight (118 pounds), even though Louis was a light heavyweight weighing 169 pounds. The smaller fighter was so fast with his hands and footwork that Louis hardly laid a glove on him. But Joe continued to work and improve. Williams and others at Brewster's, where Joe continued to train, encouraged him, told him he had the makings of a good fighter, and said he should work toward that goal.

## Winner by a Knockout

Then a memorable moment came for Louis. He recalled, "I trained hard in January of 1933, and they sent me against Otis Thomas in the Forest Athletic Club in Detroit. I took care of him with two punches. That was my first knockout."[8]

But success at fighting and the winner's twenty-five-dollar merchandise check didn't ease all of Louis's financial worries. He still boxed in canvas tennis shoes instead of leather boxing shoes, and reused his hand wraps instead of cutting them off and discarding them like most other boxers did.

## All Things Being Equal

To assure fairness in boxing, fighters fight in various divisions according to what they weigh. Strict weigh-ins are conducted before each fight and a fighter has to be at or under the prescribed weight for that division. Most of Joe Louis's fights were as a heavyweight, which is 176 pounds or more. There was no maximum for a heavyweight, but other weight classes did have strict maximum weights. There was no minimum weight—a fighter just had to be no more than the maximum weight for that class. There was nothing to prevent a confident middleweight (160 pounds) from getting into the ring with a heavyweight (176 or more).

The weight classes and the weight limits in Louis's time were as follows:

| | |
|---|---|
| Flyweight | 112 pounds |
| Bantamweight | 118 pounds |
| Featherweight | 126 pounds |
| Lightweight | 135 pounds |
| Welterweight | 147 pounds |
| Middleweight | 160 pounds |
| Light Heavyweight | 175 pounds |
| Heavyweight | unlimited |

*Louis weighs in before a 1951 fight against Andy Walker. At 207 pounds, Louis is classified as a heavyweight, as he was for most of his fights.*

## Golden Glover

Louis continued to compile an impressive record as an amateur fighter in both the Golden Gloves and Amateur Athletic Union (AAU) programs during the remainder of 1933 and into 1934. His overall amateur record was fifty victories in fifty-four bouts. Of those fifty wins, forty-three were knockouts. But one of Louis's amateur fights stood out in his memory. He fought an older, more experienced boxer named Stanley Evans. Evans's ring savvy and experience were too much for Louis, and the referee and ringside judges gave the decision to Evans at the end of the fight. Evans was the last man, amateur or pro, to defeat Louis until his twenty-eighth professional fight in 1936.

Louis avenged the loss to Evans several months later when they met in the Detroit Golden Gloves tournament. Evans tried to fight Louis the same way he did in their first match, jabbing and throwing quick combinations. But Louis was ready for him. Joe blocked many of his punches and effectively counterpunched. When the bout was over, Joe had landed considerably more punches than Evans in each round and was declared the winner. This victory made Joe Louis the amateur light heavyweight champion of Detroit.

After the fight, Louis's new trainer, George Moody, introduced the young boxer to John Roxborough. Roxborough was involved in the local numbers game, an illegal form of gambling, but his active membership and work with the Young Negroes Progressive Association and the Urban League made him a respectable member of the black community despite his gambling activities. Roxborough offered to help Louis if he promised to work hard and lead a clean life.

## Under New Management

With his mother's and stepfather's approval, Louis moved into Roxborough's home. Roxborough became Joe's manager, provided him with pocket money, and bought the young man fresh hand

*Louis poses with manager John Roxborough, who directed Louis on the path from amateur to professional fighter.*

## Chosen Profession

*With opportunities limited by the hard times of the depression, many young men turned to professions that they might not normally attempt, for example, boxing. Author Chris Mead in* Champion, *his biography of Joe Louis, explains why Louis and others tried this field.*

"Louis had chosen a difficult profession. Thousands of poor boys flooded inner-city gyms during the Depression. Dreaming of quick money, their parents played the numbers; these boys were entering a tougher lottery. Most wound up with little to show for their struggle. After a career in the ring, many moved slowly and slurred their speech, punch drunk from absorbing too many blows to the head. But a few did get rich, at least for a time. A top boxer could earn more money on a good night than the average American worker earned in a year; the heavyweight champion of the world could make more in one night than the President of the United States was paid in several years. And money was not the only reward. A popular heavyweight champion got almost as much publicity as the president and was held in higher esteem by a large percentage of the public."

*Louis embarked on his boxing career during a time when thousands of poor youths dreamed of making their fortune in the boxing ring.*

wraps for each workout and fight, good boxing shoes, and satin boxing trunks. Wilhemina Morris, a woman who would later marry Roxborough, bought Louis a terrycloth robe to wear as he entered the ring for each fight. Louis kept the robe long after he was world champion and wore it in his training camps as he prepared for his title defenses.

On June 12, 1934, Louis fought for the last time as an amateur in an intercity Golden Gloves tournament. In the future he would no longer fight for merchandise checks and trophies. As a professional, he would fight for money. In his last amateur fight, his opponent was Joe Bauer of Cleveland. The fight took place at Ford Field in Detroit. The future heavyweight champion, using a barrage of punches, put Bauer away in the first round in a little over a minute and a half. Louis used a left to the jaw followed by a right to the head in his final assault that sent Bauer sprawling to the canvas for the count of ten.

## Turning Pro

After the Bauer fight, Louis asked Roxborough if he could fight professionally so that he could use the money to support his mother and other family members. Roxy was reluctant because he thought Louis should continue to gain fighting experience as an amateur for a while longer. Roxy knew that many of the pro fighters Louis would be matched against would have much more experience, but knowing how much the boxer's family needed the income, Roxy agreed. Louis had one more request:

> I told Mr. Roxborough, "OK, I'm ready, but you have to tell my momma." Next day, I told Momma that Mr. Roxborough was coming by; she wanted to know why. She, like everybody else, respected him and appreciated everything he had been doing for me, but I held out and told her to wait and see.
>
> Mr. Roxborough had the charm and intelligence to know how to convince people. He told my momma and stepfather all the things he had talked to me about. Finally, Momma said yes, if he would make sure I lived well and led a decent Christian life.[9]

With his mother's approval, Joe Louis began a truly remarkable career—in and out of the boxing ring.

Chapter

# 2 Joe Louis, Pro Boxer

Young Joe Louis was about to embark on a career that neither he nor many others could have imagined would be as fabulously successful as it was—a career that many still consider the greatest career in heavyweight boxing.

Louis moved quickly from minor four-round fights in local clubs to main events, ten-round fights in larger arenas, to still more important fights in the boxing centers of the world—New York City and other major cities.

With his mother's blessings, Joe headed from Detroit to Chicago to begin his professional boxing career. The year was 1934, and Joe was barely twenty years old. John Roxborough wanted to introduce Joe to Julian Black, who would help manage the fighter's career. Black would work directly with Louis in Chicago while Roxborough remained in Detroit. They would split the manager's share of Louis's winnings, which would be half of whatever Joe won.

## Meet Mr. Black

Louis recalled his first meeting with Black:

> They took me over to an apartment building on Forty-sixth Street. I was to take a room in an apartment owned by Bill Bottoms. Bill was a chef. When I started training in camps, he would run the kitchen and continued to for the rest of my fighting days. First time in my life that I was going to have a room all to myself. First time in my life that I was going to know privacy and learn to love it—and, sometimes, hate it.
>
> Mr. Black looked at me hard. He was making a big investment in me and expected me to make a big investment in myself. Training would be long and hard so I would be ready. But he was going to drop most of the "string" of other fighters he managed and just concentrate on me.[10]

Black was about to devote all of his energy toward making Louis the best boxer he could be and wanted Joe to realize the type of commitment he expected in return.

## "Chappie," Meet "Chappie"

Louis immediately began a daily training routine that included running twice around Washington Park, a distance of six miles, and practicing at Trafton's gym. George Trafton, a former center for the Chicago Bears football team, owned the gym.

*Joe Louis and the men who directed his rise to fame. From left to right, Julian Black, Jack Blackburn, Joe Louis, John Roxborough, and Russell Cowan.*

Louis was introduced to his new trainer, the man who would oversee his development as a boxer. Jack Blackburn was bald and wiry and had a nasty scar that ran from the corner of his mouth up to his left ear. An ex-fighter, Blackburn had fought as a lightweight, one of the eight divisions or weight classes into which boxing is grouped. He had fought in more than one hundred bouts, winning the vast majority of them.

Blackburn wouldn't permit Louis to enter the boxing ring for a week. Because he wanted Joe to work on basic fundamentals before sparring with another boxer, he simply had Joe hit a punching bag. Blackburn held the heavy bag as Louis banged away, all the while giving Louis pointers and instruction. Joe kept up this routine for hours each day. Finally, Blackburn asked Joe to enter the practice ring against a sparring partner. Blackburn quickly saw Joe's faults.

Joe related:

> I was hitting off balance. He started correcting this by showing me how to plant my feet and punch with my whole body, not just by swinging my arm. He said people going to a fight

*The relationship between Louis and his trainer "Chappie" Blackburn was particularly close. Blackburn, in fact, served as a surrogate father to the young fighter.*

don't want to see a dancer and a clincher—they want to see a man who has the guts to stand toe-to-toe and slug it out. He said I had strength and that I could beat or knockout anybody I wanted if I planted my body in the right position. . . .

I looked at him, told him that I'd promise him and myself there would be no time wasted. With a tight little smile, Blackburn said, "OK, Chappie?" I smiled and said back, "OK, Chappie," and that's what we called each other from then on—Chappie.[11]

Although Louis never specifically spoke on the record about Chappie (Blackburn) as a surrogate or substitute father to him, in all likelihood the older trainer was a father figure for Joe. Louis never really knew his biological father, Munroe Barrow, and while he spoke well of his stepfather, Pat Brooks, there is not much evidence that they enjoyed a true father-son relationship.

Jack Blackburn was truly someone Joe could look up to. Chappie was dedicated to Joe's best interests, to making him the best boxer he could be—perhaps even the heavyweight champion of the world. Joe formed a solid partnership with his trainer and followed Blackburn's expert instruction and training without question.

Blackburn told him anecdotes about other black fighters. Blackburn told his student how black fighters were cheated at the end of their fights when their payouts were missing some of the dollars promised, how they seldom got fights against leading contenders or champions, how they were forced to lose on purpose or "throw" fights, and how former heavyweight champion Jack Johnson, with his arrogance, had made it very hard for the next generation

## The Jack Johnson Legacy

*When Jack Johnson, a black heavyweight, was world champion (1908–1915), he infuriated whites with his flamboyant behavior. White society couldn't accept that he twice married white women, drove expensive cars, and flashed diamond jewelry. Louis's managers wanted to create an image opposite of Johnson. Chris Mead, in* Champion, *tells how they did so.*

"They wanted to disassociate Louis from the memory of Jack Johnson. John Roxborough told reporters he had laid down seven rules for Louis to follow. Many papers printed Roxborough's commandments with approving comments:

1. He was never to have his picture taken alone with a white woman.
2. He was never to go into a nightclub alone.
3. There would be no soft fights.
4. There would be no fixed fights.
5. He was never to gloat over a fallen opponent.
6. He was to keep a "dead pan" expression in front of the cameras.
7. He was to live and fight clean.

The rules themselves were apocryphal, though Louis commented later that Roxborough had given him similar advice. It is clear that Roxborough aimed these rules at Johnson's negative image."

*With his arrogant, flamboyant behavior, veteran champion Jack Johnson earned a negative reputation outside the boxing ring.*

of black boxers. Jack Johnson was still in the white public's mind. Blackburn tried to instill a grim determination on Louis: He would have to be better than any white fighter just to get ahead.

As the night of Louis's first professional fight approached, Chappie told Louis again what it was like to be a black fighter. He told Louis that fighting a white man would stack the odds against him. Chappie told Joe he could not expect to win by a decision. He must score a knockout over his opponent and leave no room for doubt, or else the referee and judges would declare the white fighter the winner.

## Fourth of July Fireworks

Joe, his managers, and his trainer headed for Chicago's Bacon Casino, a fight club, on July 4, 1934. For the first time Joe was fighting as a pro in a match arranged by his managers. His opponent was a local heavyweight, Jack Kracken. Chappie did an excellent job of preparing Louis for the fight. Louis, showing explosive fists and power in his punches, quickly finished off Kracken.

Louis recalled the event:

> It was the main bout. I never had to fight "prelims" [preliminary fights] when I started because of the big build-up I had from Golden Gloves. Chappie knew this Kracken and how he fought. He told me just where to hit him to make him drop his guard. It came easy. I put Kracken out in two minutes of the first round. I hit him on the jaw when he dropped his guard to cover his stomach. I got $52 for the fight. Mr. Roxborough and Mr. Black let me keep it all.[12]

### The Role of the Black Boxer

*Louis looked up to his trainer, Jack "Chappie" Blackburn, who, as related in Louis's* Joe Louis: My Life, *was always giving the young fighter lessons for conducting himself in and out of the ring.*

"Sometimes I'd laugh when he told me about how black fighters were permitted in the ring just to make white fighters look good. They let you put up a good fight, but you dare not look better than some of the worst white boxers you were supposed to be fighting. Most importantly, he told me that sometime, somewhere, somebody was going to try to get me to throw a fight. He told me of the pitfalls. I remember him looking me dead in the eye and saying, 'I've done a lot of things I haven't been proud of, but I never threw a fight, and you won't either, 'cause I'll know, and then it's going to be you and me.' " [This was a hint that Chappie would know if Louis fixed a fight, and Louis would have to answer to him.]

*With one punch, Louis flattens opponent Eddie Simms during a 1936 fight. During his early boxing career, Louis earned a reputation for knocking out opponents.*

After the speedy and decisive knockout of Kracken, Louis added to his reputation with three quick knockouts in three more fights. Louis was becoming a knockout artist, a fighter who can quickly knock out his opponent. A true knockout artist is quite rare in boxing. He must have several kinds of powerful and damaging punches, be able to take a strong punch himself, and also be able to box well enough to avoid getting beaten. A slugger can be compared to a basketball player who intimidates with slam dunks (Shaquille O'Neal of the L.A. Lakers), a football player who piles up great yardage and scores touchdowns (Emmitt Smith of the Dallas Cowboys), or a baseball player who hits many home runs (Frank Thomas of the Chicago White Sox).

## Earning a Reputation

Fans began to label Joe as an up-and-coming fighter because of the quick way that he ended his early fights—by knockouts.

Louis wrote in "My Story":

> They [his managers] had me matched with Alex Borchuk, a tough experienced lumberjack, from Canada, in the Naval Armory. I knocked him out

### Chappie's Methods

*Louis developed a close relationship with Jack "Chappie" Blackburn, his crafty trainer. Blackburn would later become a father figure for Louis. In* Joe Louis: My Life, *Louis tells of Chappie's unorthodox, but effective, methods.*

"One day I walked in the gym, and Chappie had a red brick in his hand. He raised up his arm and it looked like he was going to hit me with it. I did what anybody would do, I ducked. Chappie laughed, 'See what I'm trying to teach you? Pretend you have a brick in your fist. Naturally, the guy's gonna duck, then you hit him with the other hand.' He [Adolph Wiater] was a 'crowder,' the first man to bring blood to my face. I decisioned him, though. The next day in the gym Chappie showed me how to beat a crowder. Catch him under the arm, spin him around, and bang him on the jaw. Nobody crowded me much after that."

> in the fourth round, but the crowd didn't know how tough this one was. This Borchuk hit me harder than any fighter before or since. He fetched one to my jaw that broke one of my back teeth.[13]

Louis continued to fight in Chicago during the late summer and early fall. A veteran local fighter from Green Bay, Wisconsin, Adolph Wiater, was his next opponent. By now Louis was fighting ten-round, main-event fights regularly. Wiater went the full ten rounds with Joe, but Louis won the decision—the referee and two ringside judges agreed that Louis was the superior boxer in the match. The match against Wiater was one of the few fights, so far, to go the full scheduled number of rounds, and Louis would later put Wiater in a class with fighters "who hurt me most." The powerful Louis continued to win by knockout, usually a quick one.

Joe was winning, and winning the way the boxing public liked. Word quickly circulated in and around Chicago about the power and the skill of the young black heavyweight. Louis's early professional unbeaten record stood at nine victories—seven of them by knockouts.

To counter a perception by sportswriters that Louis's record was achieved against mediocre fighters, Roxborough and Black were determined to match Joe with nationally known fighter Stanley Poreda, a tough slugger and former dockworker from Hoboken, New Jersey. Poreda had a reputation as an aggressive, brawling fighter who swarmed all over his opponents. His punishing style was supposed to be a good test for the rising young Louis. Although Poreda looked to be a worthy opponent, the fight turned into one of Joe's easiest.

As Poreda moved in, Louis connected with a crashing right to the jaw and the "hot fighter from the East" was just another first-round knockout victim. Louis had done what he wanted to do. He won the fight convincingly and gave credibility to his managers' claim that he was going to be a contender for the championship in the future.

Many fight promoters and sportswriters, however, remained skeptical of Joe's skills. Joe's managers arranged for him to fight Charley Massera. Massera was an aggressive fighter from Monongahela, Pennsylvania, a mill town just outside of Pittsburgh that would become better known in the future as the hometown of football star Joe Montana.

This fight was in Chicago Stadium, the site of many major fights and other athletic events. Louis knocked out Massera in the third round and received his biggest check to date, twelve hundred dollars. Louis used this money to pay back the relief money that his family received during the depression.

Louis continued to fight nationally known and nationally ranked opponents. His last fight of 1934 was with Los Angeles heavyweight Lee Ramage. The fight would be in Chicago.

## Romantic Interest

While training for the Ramage fight, an event occurred that would change Joe's future. Like any young man in his late teens, Louis developed an interest in young women. He related:

> A lot of people came in to watch me train. Out of the corner of my eye, I saw the most beautiful girl I'd ever seen. I found out later that the only reason she came to the gym was that an insurance executive friend of hers had promised to introduce her to "the next heavyweight champion of the world." She saw me work out, but I didn't get a chance to meet her. I had an interview with sportswriter Al Monroe of the *Chicago Defender*, a black newspaper. She was working there as a secretary. I found out her name was Marva Trotter.[14]

Although Louis was too shy to ask Marva for a date after seeing her at the newspaper office, he wouldn't forget about her.

On December 14, Louis decked Ramage in the third round of their fight. As Chappie instructed him to do, he backed his more experienced opponent into a corner and dropped him with a hard left to the body followed by a powerful right to the jaw.

To celebrate the victory and the fact that he remained undefeated after a dozen pro fights, Joe wanted to have a party, and he wanted to invite Marva:

> "Chappie," I said, "I'm going to have a party and I want you to invite that Marva who came to the gym." She came to the party with her sister Gladys. I liked her; she was a real lady. We sat there talking about things we wanted to do in life. She was attending the Vogue School of Designing of Chicago and wanted to be a great designer. She also was taking courses in English at the University of Chicago, and working as a secretary at the newspaper. Marva was the first real ambitious woman I ever met, and she was only eighteen years old.[15]

## Back to Boxing

Louis took the money from the Ramage fight to Detroit to celebrate the Christmas holidays in style with his family and friends but was back in training for his next scheduled bout on January 4, 1935. His opponent, Patsy Perroni of Cleveland, was also a promising young heavyweight, although he had more experience than Joe. Perroni was a tough fighter. Louis's punches knocked him down three times during the fight, but Perroni would not stay down. Several times Perroni exchanged punches with Louis, staggering the young black fighter. But Louis was the winner by a decision after ten rounds. By being able to fight a full half hour (ten 3-minute rounds) and not be overcome by Perroni's experience in the ring, Joe proved to himself and to his managers, trainer, and critics that he could take it as well as give it out. The fight paid Louis four thousand dollars—a handsome sum for thirty minutes' work for a twenty-year-old during the hard times of the Great Depression.

All the time Louis was fighting, he was adding muscle to his frame by his training,

*Louis and Marva Trotter walk along a Harlem street in 1935. Trotter attracted Louis's attention a year earlier, and they soon after became romantically involved.*

### Namesakes

*According to Jack Clary in* Great Teams, Great Years—Cleveland Browns, *that NFL team is named after Joe "the Brown Bomber" Louis. When the team was first created in 1946, Panthers was suggested as the team name, but there were problems.*

"The name Panthers already had prior ownership. It was the name of a semi-pro team near Cleveland. Brown [head coach Paul Brown] ordered some inquiries made and discovered that such a team not only existed but worse than that, had been chronic losers.

'Forget the name,' he [Brown] told team owner Mickey McBride. 'I won't have my team associated with a loser.'

So McBride staged a contest and, according to Brown, the trend shifted toward naming the team after other champions.

'Joe Louis was the best known champion at the time, and we received a lot of entries suggesting we name the team the Brown Bombers,' said Brown. 'So we decided to shorten the name and call the team the Browns.' "

daily diet, and regular workouts. For his next fight he would weigh 194 pounds.

## What's in a Name?

Joe was now well enough known that reporters covering his fights felt compelled to come up with a suitable nickname. Sportswriters in Louis's time, much like today's writers and broadcasters, were great for giving athletes nicknames—the more colorful, the better. Joe's most popular and enduring nickname was "the Brown Bomber." Ironically, it wasn't a writer who came up with the name. Louis set the record straight on how he got the nickname:

> They called me "the Brown Bomber" and it got out that the writers thought that up, but they didn't. Mr. Roxborough was talking with Scotty Monteith, who had been a fighter and was then a fight manager. When Mr. Monteith went home he got an idea. He called Mr. Roxborough on the telephone. He said, "I got a good name for your boy. You call him 'the Brown Bomber.' " That's how it was.[16]

Louis had other nicknames, too: the Dark Destroyer, the Alabama Assassin, the Detroit Destroyer, the Michigan Mauler, and the Sepia Socker. For better or worse, probably better, the Brown Bomber stuck.

Although Louis was gaining a fine reputation in the Midwest, his management

*Louis affectionately drapes his arm over "Uncle Mike" Jacobs. Jacobs's shrewd tactics as a promoter rocketed Louis to fame.*

team of Roxborough, Black, and Blackburn thought Joe needed to gain more national exposure. They wanted Louis to fight in New York City. New York was the center of the nation's media in those days—newspapers, magazines, and radio. It was also the center of the sport of boxing. Because their contacts were mainly in the Midwest, Louis's managers could make little headway in cracking the important New York market. They needed a plan that would get their boxer exposure in New York City.

## Setting the Stage

New York was vital to Joe's future.

> In the Depression, few out-of-town newspapers could afford to send reporters of their own to cover training camps and fights. New York writers had syndicated columns that were reprinted as far away as Seattle. In addition, sportswriters in other cities read the works of the New York writers, borrowed information from them, and emulated their styles. The combination of Jacobs's press releases [the fight promoter hired press agents to cover the training camps of Louis and his opponents] and the widespread reprinting and imitation of the big city writers ensured that press coverage of Louis was basically uniform throughout the rest of the country and remarkably repetitious.[17]

## Ticket to New York

Louis's managers struck a deal with Mike Jacobs, known throughout boxing as "Uncle Mike," a promoter on a grand scale.

He formed Twentieth Century Sporting Club to compete with the promoters who denied him the use of Madison Square Garden, the mecca of boxing at the time. Jacobs was a controversial man. Many observers thought of him, just as they did other fight promoters, as a parasite—not doing much of anything and living off the efforts of those in the boxing ring who put their careers and sometimes their lives on the line. In the opinion of many, Don King is thought of in that light today.

Perhaps Louis himself best judged Jacobs's role:

> There has been a lot of talk about Mike Jacobs using me for a sucker, but that's all wrong. If it wasn't for Mike Jacobs I never would have got to be champion. He arranged for me to get a crack at the title, and he never once asked me to do anything wrong or phony in the ring.[18]

Jacobs set up a fight between Natie Brown and Louis in Detroit. For the Louis-Brown fight in late March, Jacobs hired a private railroad car to take many New York writers to see young Joe Louis box. To stress the importance of the fight, Roxborough and Black told Louis that this fight could be a stepping-stone to a fight that could pay $100,000 or more. For someone who thought a couple of thousand dollars was big money, this sum was almost unimaginable.

Brown, a hard, experienced fighter and the eighth-ranked heavyweight contender in the world, was thought of as a "wide open" fighter, but in this match he wasn't. Instead of leaving his hands down and leaving himself open to Louis's punches, Brown crouched low and offered no real target for Joe to hit.

Louis remembered:

> Natie Brown fooled me. He didn't come out "open." He came out all covered up and it was hard to find a hole to shoot at. I got through a few times. He cut pretty easy and I worked on his eyes, but I couldn't put him away. He stayed away from me for ten rounds.[19]

Louis was the winner by decision and was impressive enough in gaining the decision to win over the New York writers. His national reputation as a legitimate contender grew rapidly. New York was still some time and distance away, though. Louis completed a quick succession of five fights that he won by knockouts. He would not fight again until June 25, when he would take on former heavyweight champion Primo Carnera outdoors at Yankee Stadium—in New York City.

Chapter

# 3 The Big Apple

Legend says that early jazz musicians nicknamed New York City the "Big Apple." It was a respectful term paying tribute to New York's status as the center of much of what was happening and much of what was important. Outside of filmmaking in Hollywood, New York was the nation's entertainment center. The success of the New York Yankees and New York Giants in baseball made it an important sports center. With Wall Street, it was a business center. Leading medical research and treatment in New York's many famous hospitals made it a medical mecca. Other fields were also represented at the top by what was going on in New York. To be really accepted as a success, you had to be successful in New York.

## Uncle Mike

For these reasons, boxing well in New York was important to Louis's career. Without a promoter of Uncle Mike Jacobs's stature and ability, Louis might have taken a longer road to the bouts that would lead to a heavyweight title fight—or he may never have had the opportunity at all.

The shrewd Jacobs obtained the backing of the powerful Hearst newspaper chain, a valuable bit of public relations, by pledging a portion of the Louis-Carnera fight proceeds to the Hearst Milk Fund. This pet charity of Mrs. William Randolph

*The influential William Randolph Hearst and his wife, who backed Louis in exchange for proceeds from his fight with Primo Carnera. Exposure in the Hearst newspaper chain drew much publicity for Louis.*

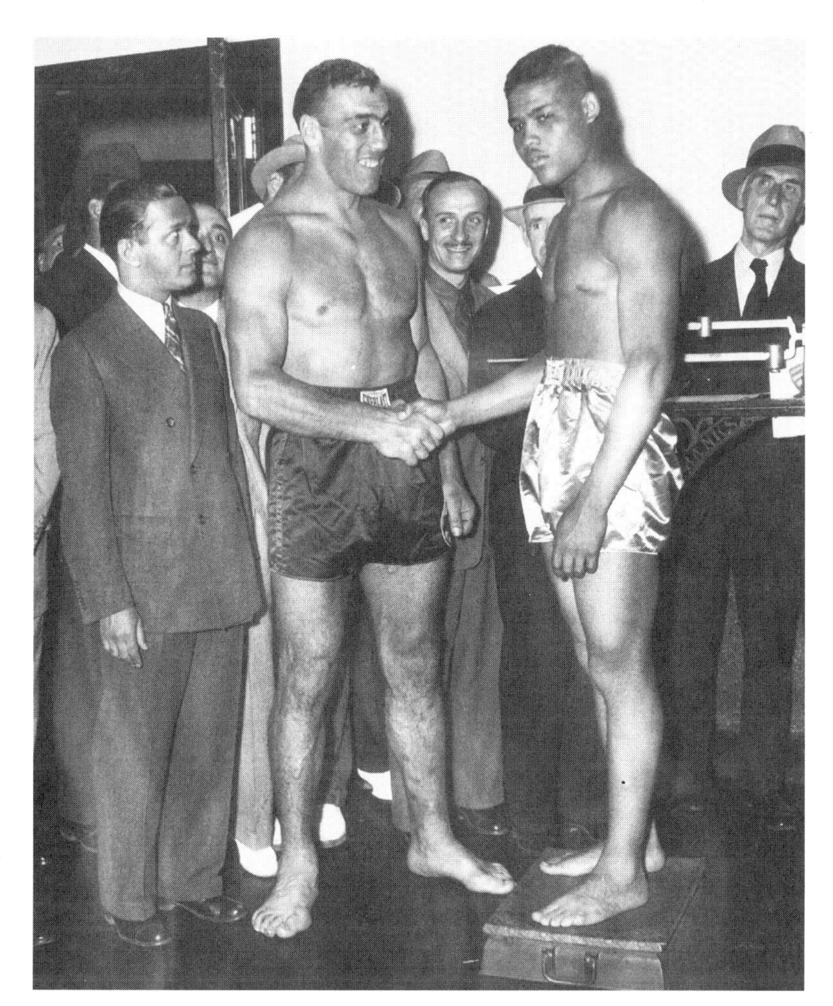

*Primo Carnera shakes hands with Louis as the boxers weigh-in before they climb through the ropes. Fans and sports commentators noted Carnera's gargantuan size—five inches taller and sixty pounds heavier than Louis.*

Hearst paid for milk for school lunches for New York's many underprivileged schoolchildren. The Hearst backing included many prefight stories about the upcoming match—publicity that drew much interest and would have cost a small fortune if the same newspaper space had to be purchased as advertising.

Before Louis started serious training for the Carnera fight, he surprised his mother by buying her a home and giving it to her on Easter Sunday 1935. It was a four-bedroom house in the 2100 block of McDougal Avenue in Detroit. The house cost nine thousand dollars, and Louis paid in cash with money from his most recent fights.

## Training for Carnera

Because the six-foot, six-inch, 260-pound Carnera was so much bigger than Louis, or almost any other fighter of the time, Louis's handlers used special training methods to prepare their fighter for his New York City debut. Chappie Blackburn carried out a nationwide search to find sparring partners for Joe. They had to be more than willing to step into the ring with Louis and take his punishing blows; they had to be big men.

Louis said of Blackburn, "He figured if I was going to take on a giant, he would train me with giants."[20]

Each of Louis's sparring partners, Seal Harris, Ace Clark, and Leonard Dixon, approximated Carnera's size. Harris and Clark were almost a head taller than Louis. Dixon was a little taller than Joe, but much more "beefy." Next to these men, Louis looked like a middleweight instead of a leading heavyweight contender.

## World Politics

About the time Louis was getting ready to fight Primo Carnera, things were happening throughout the world that would draw special attention to the bout between the young, up-and-coming black American fighter and the giant Italian who had once been world champ.

The fight took on symbolic meaning when Italy's Fascist dictator Benito Mussolini invaded Ethiopia, a small country across the Mediterranean Sea. Ethiopia was one of the few independent black nations on earth. Because Louis was black, he became a symbol for nearly all blacks and many others who sympathized with the Ethiopians. Carnera, not necessarily by his own choosing, represented the forces of Mussolini's Fascist regime. More than just another boxing match, this fight was looked upon by many as a symbolic match between good versus evil. If nothing else, it solidified Louis as a symbol of his race—to blacks and to white society in general.

## The Fight

In introducing the fighters, ring announcer Harry Balogh addressed the political situation when he asked that "the thought in your mind and the feeling in your heart be that regardless of race, creed, or color, let us all say, may the better man emerge victorious."[21] Balogh's statement was a very unusual prefight announcement. It was a public—but somewhat insincere—attempt to ask people to put aside their political feelings and enjoy the boxing match as strictly an athletic contest. Few saw this match as just another fight.

Although Carnera had been the heavyweight champ, he was generally thought of as one of the worst boxers to ever hold the title. His boxing career was quite accidental. He had been a carnival "strongman" when some exploitive boxing promoters thought that anyone that big and strong could become a boxer. He won the title from Jack Sharkey at the time when new heavyweight champions defended their titles infrequently and were content to stay out of the ring for a year or more and just be "heavyweight champion of the world." They really didn't need to do much more. Public appearances, for which they were paid handsomely, provided a safer way to generate income. Carnera didn't hold his title long, but at least he could say when he stepped into the ring with Louis that he had once worn the heavyweight crown.

Giving away five inches in height and sixty pounds in weight, Louis climbed into the ring on the evening of June 25, 1935. Sixty thousand fans crowded into Yankee Stadium. Because it was summer, the outdoor site, which could seat this large crowd, was chosen over Madison Square Garden, which could only seat fifteen thousand. On hand were four hundred sportswriters, the largest delegation to attend a fight since Jack Dempsey, another American heavyweight champion, was in his prime in the 1920s.

The fight was rather uneventful for the first four rounds, but with less than a minute left in the fifth, Louis hit Carnera with a short right. When Carnera tried to clinch, Louis actually picked him up and threw him aside. Louis remembered, "That's when he spoke to me for the only time in the fight. He said, 'Oh . . . oh . . . oh.' His eyes bulged and then he said, 'I should be doing this to you.' "[22]

In the sixth round, Louis hit Carnera with a right hand that caused blood to appear at the side of his mouth. Another right sent the giant to the canvas. Still another of Louis's mighty rights knocked Carnera down again. Louis used a left-right combination to floor Carnera for the third and last time. The final moments of the fight saw Louis reduce Carnera to the point where he only was left with his courage and ability to absorb punishment. As he got up, Carnera actually took a step backward, his arms at his side and a glassy-eyed look on his face. When Carnera put his left hand on the top ring rope for support, referee Arthur Donovan stepped between Louis and Carnera and waved his

*Louis pummels opponent Carnera during their highly publicized fight in June 1935.*

arms. This signaled the fight was over and Louis was the winner by a technical knock-out (TKO).

Louis later said, "He never hurt me once. I felt ready for any heavyweight in the world—Jimmy Braddock, Max Baer, anybody."[23]

## Misconception

Much was made of Louis's boxing ability in the weeks following the Carnera fight. Reflective of the racial attitudes of the time, sportswriters mentioned Louis's "natural ability" and "jungle instincts." Grantland Rice, perhaps the most-read sportswriter in this age of syndicated columnists, once wrote a poem about Louis that likened him to a prehistoric jungle stalker. Actually, Louis was not a "natural" boxer. He was strong, but slow afoot. His hand speed and agile footwork that would be cited so often as his career took off were the result of countless hours and days spent in the gym, skipping rope, shadowboxing, hitting the speed bag, slugging the heavy bag, running near-marathon distances daily, and listening to the wise instructions of Chappie Blackburn. If Louis was a natural, he made himself one through very hard work and serious dedication to his profession.

Once Louis proved himself so decisively against Carnera, many fighters, fight managers, and cities wanted to be part of Joe Louis's next fight. Some cities

### A Great Example

*Steve Stephanou boxed collegiately at Bucknell University from 1935 to 1938 when college boxing was a high-profile sport. He saw Louis fight Tommy Farr in Yankee Stadium on August 30, 1937. In a personal interview, he related the following:*

"My boxing career at Bucknell was from 1935 to 38. So Joe Louis was relatively young while I was boxing. But we, the boxing team at Bucknell, were well aware of him from about the time I arrived on campus. He was a leading contender before he was champ my senior year. He was so good you couldn't ignore him.

Joe really got my attention when he defeated Primo Carnera in 1935. Now, Da Preem [how Carnera was referred to by many] wasn't much of a fighter. In fact, he was really a circus strongman. He couldn't lick a postage stamp. But he was big. For Louis to maul him like he did in their fight, Joe had to be a great boxer. He proved that later.

I don't think we were aware of role models in those days, but he was a great example to follow. We all would like to have been as good as Joe Louis was then."

*Max Baer lands a powerful blow on Louis, who nevertheless defeated Baer by a knockout in the fourth round.*

were prepared to offer their stadiums or arenas at no charge. Promoters and fighters all wanted part of the glory, and cash, that could come from fighting a prime contender.

Jacobs, having once tasted the success of a New York fight, was leaning toward Louis's fighting in the Big Apple again. Roxborough and Black convinced Jacobs to return to the city where Louis's professional career first drew wide acclaim, Chicago.

Harry "Kingfish" Levinsky was to be Joe's next opponent. Levinsky had a reputation as a solid puncher, a strong hitter, and a slugger. Louis's handlers reasoned that a fight with Levinsky would show the one thing missing from the Carnera fight—that Louis could take a heavy punch.

The Louis-Levinsky fight was set for August 7 at Chicago's Comiskey Park, home field of baseball's White Sox. Whether the fight proved anything, except that Louis was very good, is questionable. He threw less than ten punches to knock out Levinsky in the opening moments of the first round. For his efforts, Louis's share of the purse was fifty-three thousand dollars. This sum added nicely to the sixty-thousand dollars he earned for the Carnera fight. Louis was on his way to fame and fortune.

## A Big Step in the Big Apple

Louis was scheduled to fight Max Baer on September 24. Again, the location of the

*Louis took time out from training for his fight with Max Baer to marry Marva Trotter. The wedding took place just hours before the big fight.*

fight was Yankee Stadium. Baer, like Carnera, was much bigger than Louis and a former heavyweight champion. Baer was listed at six feet, six inches and 260 pounds, and had lost the heavyweight title to Jimmy Braddock only a few months before he was to fight Louis. He was considered a much more serious challenge to Louis's pursuit of the heavyweight crown than Carnera had been.

Louis's preparation for the bout did not prevent him from taking time to court Marva Trotter. The attractive young couple had been seeing each other for a couple of years, and Marva's family gave them permission to marry. Marva's brother, the Reverend Walter Trotter, performed the ceremony at the Harlem apartment of a friend just hours before Louis left for Yankee Stadium to fight Baer. It was quite a social event. Louis recalled:

> The halls were filled with reporters and cameramen, and lots of neighbors. I couldn't come through the crowd to Lucille Armstead's apartment, where Marva was staying, so I came down the fire escape from the fifth floor. We had the wedding at Lucille's place.[24]

Louis then went to fight. Marva was also there. The new Mrs. Joseph Louis Barrow had a ringside seat when announcer Joe Humphreys introduced the fighters:

> We'll be brief because you want action, and I'm here for that purpose. Main event. Fifteen rounds. Principals. Presenting the sensational Californian and former world heavyweight champion, Max Baer! His worthy opponent, the new sensational pugilistic product . . .

> although colored . . . he stands out in the same class as Jack Johnson and Sam Langford . . . the idol of his people . . . none other than . . . Joe . . . Louis![25]

Louis soundly pummeled Baer. By the second round, Baer was bleeding and confused. He even hit Louis twice after the bell, but Louis just stared at him. Twice in round three Louis floored the giant Baer, once for the nine count and again at the end of the round when the bell saved Baer after only a four count.

In the fourth round, Baer was on his last wobbly legs. Louis continued to hammer away, hitting Baer with combinations, but scoring mostly with what many people considered a deadly weapon—his hard right hand. Baer forced a clinch that the referee broke. Then Louis forced him into the ropes and hit him with a devastating right and left to the jaw. Baer's knees buckled, and he was down. He got to one knee at the count of six. It looked as though he could get up, but he didn't. Baer was still on one knee at the count of ten, counted out. Louis was the victor by a knockout.

Baer was asked about being counted out while on one knee. He may have lost the fight but not his sense of humor, as he replied, "I could have struggled up once more, but when I get executed, people are going to have to pay more than twenty-five dollars a seat to watch it."[26]

Joe and Marva had no time for a honeymoon, but they did manage to get back to Chicago for a few weeks after the Baer fight. A huge crowd, estimated at ten thousand, gathered in the street in front of their home. Only an appearance on the porch by the celebrated newlyweds could quiet the crowd. While out on the porch, Joe tossed his hat to the crowd. A near brawl resulted as many in the crowd struggled for the souvenir.

## Madison Square Garden—Finally

Louis would not fight again in 1935 until December 13. The fight would be in boxing's "mecca," Madison Square Garden in New York City. Louis was going to fight Paulino Uzcudun. Uzcudun, who earlier in the year had gone twelve rounds with former heavyweight champion Max Schmeling, was a formidable foe. Uzcudun was still another building block in Louis's climb to the championship. Uzcudun was no pushover; Louis said, "This Uzcudun was a croucher, very hard to hit."[27]

True to Blackburn's description of Uzcudun, the boxer came at Louis in a pronounced crouch. He was bent at the waist with his arms covering his face. He was so low his forearms were parallel to the ring floor.

For four rounds Louis jabbed away at Uzcudun. But the crafty veteran's gloves and arms always seemed to be in the way of Louis's punches. Then Louis took a step back and Uzcudun separated his arms from in front of his face to see where Louis was. It was a fatal mistake. Faster than you can read this, Louis took full advantage of the opening and lashed out with what many observers called the most devastating and damaging blow they ever saw in a boxing ring. The force of Louis's right lifted the two-hundred-pound Uzcudun off his feet and dumped him halfway across the ring. Uzcudun's face was cut from the force of Louis's punch. Louis said, "I was glad the referee stopped

## Growin' Up with Joe

*Like many rural southern blacks of the depression era, noted author and poet Maya Angelou listened to Joe Louis fights on the radio. In Angelou's case, the radio was at a general store, owned by her uncle in rural Arkansas. The mood of the crowd rose and fell with how well Louis was doing in the ring. From her highly successful* I Know Why the Caged Bird Sings, *she describes the experience.*

"The men in the store stood away from the walls and at attention. Women greedily clutched the babes on their laps while on the porch the shufflings and smiles, flirtings and pinching of a few minutes before were gone. This might be the end of the world. If Joe lost we were back in slavery and beyond help. It would be true, the accusations that we were lower types of human beings. Only a little higher than apes. True that we were stupid and ugly and lazy and dirty and, unlucky and worst of all, that God himself hated us and ordained us to be hewers of wood and drawers of water, forever and ever, world without end.

We didn't breathe. We didn't hope. We waited.

'He's off the ropes, ladies and gentlemen. He's moving towards the center of the ring.' There was no time to be relieved. The worst might still happen.

'And now it looks like Joe is mad. He's caught Carnera with a left hook to the head and a right to the head. It's a left jab to the body and another left to the head. . . . The fight's over, ladies and gentlemen. Here he [the referee] is. He's got the Brown Bomber's hand. He's holding it up. The winner . . . Joe Louis.' "

*In another passage of the book, Angelou describes the pride blacks everywhere took in Joe's accomplishments.*

"The last inch of space was filled, yet people continued to wedge themselves along the walls of the store. Uncle Willie had turned the radio up to its last notch so that the youngsters on the porch wouldn't miss a word. Women sat on kitchen chairs, dining room chairs, stools and upturned wooden boxes, small shelves or on each other. As I pushed my way into the store I wondered if the announcer gave any thought to the fact that he was addressing as 'ladies and gentlemen' all the Negroes around the world who sat sweating and praying, glued to [the radio]."

the fight."[28] It was a TKO for Louis. Louis's punch drove two of Uzcudun's teeth through his lower lip, and after sitting in his dressing room for twenty minutes after the fight, Uzcudun fell over when he tried to get up to take a shower.

An interested observer at Louis's prefight training camp in Lakewood, New Jersey, and at ringside for the Uzcudun fight was Max Schmeling, the German who held the heavyweight title from 1930 to 1932. A Louis-Schmeling fight was near, and Schmeling wanted to see what he was up against. He told reporters after the Louis-Uzcudun match that he "had noticed something,"[29] a flaw in Louis's defense.

## Tuning Up

Before Schmeling would have a chance to use what he learned watching Louis train and fight, Louis had a date with a South Dakota farmer turned boxer, Charley Retzlaff. The twenty-eight-year-old Retzlaff had a powerful right, something Louis also possessed, but Retzlaff did not have much of a chance to stop Louis's climb to the top of the heavyweight division.

> On January 17 at Chicago Stadium [an indoor arena] . . . 14,106 fight fans braved a raging blizzard to see Louis and paid $67,826.66. When the bell rang Retzlaff rushed out to meet Louis and threw a hard right, landing on the shoulder [of Louis] and another on the hip of Joe. Louis shot a hard left hook. . . . Down went Charley. He got up at seven, almost helpless. . . . Joe sent a barrage of blows, then a terrific right to the chin! A first-round KO . . . 1-minute, 25 seconds. His 23rd.[30]

A clause in the Louis-Schmeling contract prevented either fighter from entering matches before their mid-June bout. Louis and Marva welcomed the break in the training/fighting routine, but still felt they couldn't take a honeymoon trip. Louis said, "Marva and me had to stay pretty close to the house. When we went out, we drew crowds."[31]

Chapter

# 4 The First Schmeling Fight

As the fight with Max Schmeling drew near, it was evident to most followers of boxing that Joe Louis was truly the uncrowned heavyweight champion of the world. *Ring* magazine, a popular monthly magazine of the time and the semiofficial voice of the sport, ranked Louis top in his class in 1935. He was ranked even higher than the actual title holder, Jim Braddock. Nat Fleischer, publisher of the boxing magazine, backed the ranking by awarding Joe a gold belt as *Ring*'s Number One Boxer of the Year, 1935. Louis clearly was ready for a crack at the championship, and a great number of those who followed boxing thought he would make the most of the opportunity.

Schmeling returned to Germany to train, taking films of the Louis-Uzcudun fight with him. Schmeling noticed in that fight that Louis dropped his left hand as he was about to throw a hard right-hand punch. This observation would prove to be valuable for Schmeling.

Louis had a little matter to take care of before going into training camp. He went to Hollywood to make a quick, low-budget motion picture entitled *The Spirit of Youth.* According to Joe, "It was supposed to be

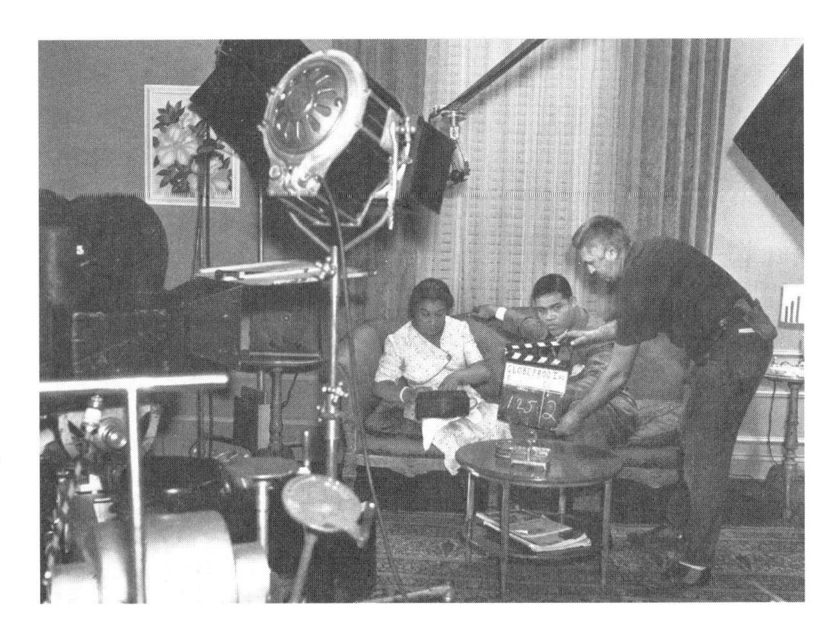

*Louis stars in the motion picture* The Spirit of Youth, *a low-budget picture that portrayed a rags-to-riches story similar to Louis's life.*

about a young, poor boy who started out as a dishwasher and wound up champion of the world. I guess it was supposed to be something like my life story."[32]

## Off to Camp

Louis trained at a new location in Lakewood, New Jersey, because in Louis's words, "My managers figured Lakewood could accommodate more visitors."[33] But training to fight Max Schmeling was more than a matter of changing locations, and Louis was not as serious as he should have been. But who could blame him? He had just turned twenty-two years old on May 13. He was ranked number one in the world. He was a heavy favorite, and there was no shortage of friends and well-wishers to tell him how great he was. Most fans agreed that in a matter of time, a short time, Joe Louis would become heavyweight champion of the world.

To add to the distraction, Marva was at the training camp, and Louis even brought his golf clubs with him. He also brought a few extra pounds. After weighing 196 when he fought Carnera, he was 216 when he got to camp to train for the Schmeling fight. And the oddsmakers didn't help his complacency when they installed him as a ten-to-one favorite over the German ex-champion.

## The Master Race

Like the Carnera bout, the Schmeling fight had its symbolic side. World War II continued to take shape in Europe. Hitler was making bold moves, annexing territories, and imprisoning people (especially Jews) simply because of their race and religion. The 1936 Olympics were to be staged in Berlin, and Hitler wanted the games to be a showcase of how his Nazis were a "super race."

The political symbolism of a black American fighting a German, with Nazi backing, was not lost on Hitler. This fight could show the world the correctness of Hitler's thinking. It would only add to what he expected to demonstrate at the Olympic Games.

While Hitler's and Nazi Germany's hopes were riding on Schmeling, American sportswriters weren't impressed with the German boxer. Bob Broeg, a respected St. Louis writer, wrote:

> You couldn't take Max seriously. Since fumbling the title to [Jack] Sharkey four years previously, he had gone to the post only six times, and had been stopped by Max Baer, decisioned by Steve Hamas, and held to a draw by that old chopping block Paulino [Uzcudun]. Taking the thirty year old German in stride would be a logical, though important, stunt before [Louis] faced [champion Jim] Braddock.[34]

## In the Ring

The fight was scheduled for Thursday, June 18, but at the weigh-in officials announced a postponement because of a heavy rain. The bout was to be outside at Yankee Stadium, which could accommodate a crowd of up to eighty-five thousand, but the rain delay reduced attendance.

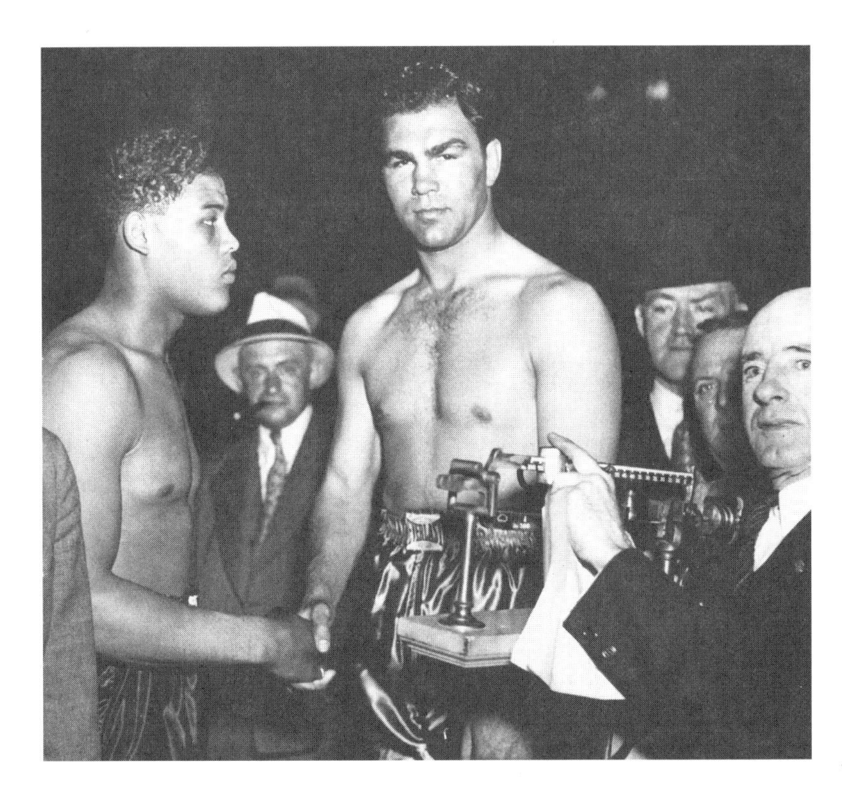

*Louis meets his German opponent Max Schmeling moments before their bout in June 1936.*

The one-day postponement resulted in only forty thousand people turning out for the fight.

Louis recalled Chappie's instructions: "Don't go for the knockout right away. Keep jabbing him off balance so he can't get the right hand in, and for God's sake keep your left arm high."[35]

When the bell rang to start the fight Schmeling came out in a severe crouch. He tucked his chin behind his left shoulder and held his left arm high—something Louis should have done with his own chin—to protect himself. Louis worked his jab as Schmeling didn't seem to take any evasive measures. He took probing punches from Louis to avoid the more damaging right. Louis nearly closed Schmeling's eye in round one. Louis was confident at the end of the opening round as he went back to his corner, telling Chappie, "Max was a pushover; I could get him anytime with a left hook."[36]

## The Difficult Lesson

In the second round, Louis ignored his trainer's advice and dropped his left arm. Schmeling reacted with a hard right to the jaw; Louis stayed on his feet, although he was hurt by the unexpected and smashing punch. In the third, Louis worked Schmeling's body successfully. Round four saw Louis open a cut under his opponent's right eye, but Schmeling surprised him with a stinging right that knocked Louis off his feet. Louis had never been knocked down as a professional boxer, although he had been dropped several times as an amateur. Louis popped right up at the count of two, but said, "To be honest, I never fully recovered from that blow."[37]

In the fifth round, Louis got tagged on the jaw with a right-handed punch that Schmeling started to throw before the bell rang to end the round, but landed after the bell sounded. There was nothing illegal or unsportsmanlike about the punch. Schmeling couldn't stop it in midair. He was in his punching motion before the bell sounded. The punch just happened to land a split second after the first sound of the bell. Regardless, it would only add to Louis's problems.

Schmeling used the sixth round to stagger Louis further. And near the end of the round, the German boxer landed another heavy right to Joe's head that sent him back to his corner in a bit of a fog.

Louis was so fuzzy that he fought on instinct alone. Twice the referee warned him for throwing low blows at Schmeling; twice he had rounds taken away from him because of those low blows.

## Down and Out

Louis seemed to rally slightly in the tenth, but the blows he landed didn't seem to have any lasting effect on Schmeling. In the eleventh, Schmeling landed more right hands, and in the twelfth the end came. Still more rights from Schmeling finished Louis at two minutes and twenty-nine seconds in the round.

Louis was soundly defeated and totally humiliated. His mother, who had come to the fight from Detroit, left in the early rounds when it appeared that Joe might not be the winner. His wife would have left, but a women's magazine writer kept asking questions for an article, and she couldn't get away. Joe's stepbrother, Pat Brooks,

*Schmeling unleashes a flurry of hard punches that Louis fails to dodge. Schmeling's blows were so fierce that they left Louis fuzzy and disoriented.*

wanted Chappie to "throw in the towel," a signal to stop the fight. It didn't happen.

Louis recalled his emotions:

> I barely remember being helped back to my dressing room by my attendants and the police. Next thing I know, I was sitting on my dressing table and crying like I don't think I ever did before. It seemed at that moment I would just die. Chappie [Blackburn] and Roxy [Roxborough] and Julian [Black] comforted me as best they could. Chappie told me not to worry, I'd do better next time, and everything happens for the best.[38]

## The Aftermath

As much as Louis meant to black Americans, the news of his defeat was shocking to most people. "Riots"—people just roaming the streets and causing disturbances—started in Chicago's "Little Harlem" section, and in Harlem itself, "a young girl [attempted] to drink poison in a corner drugstore."[39] The shock was not confined to the black community.

Baseball writer Robert W. Creamer wrote:

> I liked Louis because he was such a good fighter. I was stunned when Louis was kayoed by Schmeling. I was thirteen and I lost a quarter on that fight to my grandmother, who admired the way Schmeling kept in shape by chopping down trees. A quarter was a lot of money to me at that age and at that time. I listened to the fight on the radio—she didn't—and when it was over I went to her room and paid her the quarter, which, to her everlasting credit, she accepted. I mean, a bet's a bet. And I still liked Louis.[40]

*Schmeling stunned the boxing world with his knockout of Louis, who had been hailed as a ten-to-one favorite over Schmeling.*

### A Sad Song

*Joe Louis's loss to Max Schmeling in 1936 had an effect on many Americans, but perhaps no group was affected more profoundly than black Americans. In Chris Mead's* Champion, *he recounts torch singer Lena Horne's reaction to the loss. (In later years Miss Horne was romantically linked to the boxer.)*

"Until that night I had no idea of the strength of my identification with Joe Louis.

We had the radio on behind the grandstand and during the breaks we crowded around it to hear the fight. I was near hysteria toward the end of the fight when he was being so badly beaten and some of the men in the band were crying. . . . Joe was the one invincible Negro, the one who stood up to the white man and beat him down with his fists. He in a sense carried so many of our hopes, maybe even dreams of vengeance. But this night he was just another Negro getting beaten by a white man. . . . My mother was furious with me for getting hysterical. 'How dare you?' she screamed. 'You have a performance. The show must go on. Why, you don't even know this man.'

'I don't care, I don't care,' I yelled back. 'He belongs to all of us.' "

In Germany, the Nazi regime rejoiced at Schmeling's triumph. Writer Duff Hart-Davis described the boxer's return:

> Already a popular sporting figure in Germany, and a friend of Joseph Goebbels [a high Nazi official], Schmeling became a national hero overnight. Returning home on the zeppelin *Hindenburg*, he found himself feted and invited to meet the Fuhrer [Hitler]. As the airship arrived in Frankfurt on June 29, Schmeling was allowed to disembark as soon as it was on the ground. Once on the ground, he found his wife, the dashing German film star, Annie Ondra, and his mother, both of whom were flown to meet him in a special plane arranged by Goebbels. There was also a Nazi band, and a posse of party officials, as well as prominent sportsmen from Germany. After a reception, Schmeling was driven through the streets of Frankfurt, which were lined by cheering crowds. He arrived at Town Hall, where he was welcomed by the mayor of the city and appeared later on the balcony of the municipal building before a vast throng of people—after which he was hastened to Berlin for tea with the Fuhrer.[41]

At home, George Lee summed up the feeling of the black community toward Louis's loss: "The shock stunned the

### A Major Setback

*Before he became a controversial U.S. congressman, Adam Clayton Powell Jr. was a well-known black leader in the 1930s. He put the Louis loss in perspective in an article he wrote for the* New York Amsterdam News.

"Along came the Brown Bomber, Death in the Evening, and our racial morale took a sky high leap that broke every record from Portland [Maine] to Pasadena [California]. Surely the new day was just around the corner. . . .

Then along came the sudden fall of Addis Ababa [in Ethiopia, which was under attack from Italy] and the Yankee Stadium fiasco [a reference to Louis losing the fight to Schmeling] and something died. Gone today is the jauntiness, the careless abandon, the spring in our stride—we're just shufflin' along."

sports world. Thirteen million Negroes couldn't believe their idol had fallen. It was a sad night in Harlem and all over the country.[42]

It's safe to say that many members of the white community, those who looked on Louis first as an American and those who sensed the evil of Hitler's Nazis, joined blacks in their disappointment.

Former champion Jack Dempsey, though, was not sympathetic to Louis. He said:

> Schmeling exposed the fact that Louis has a glass jaw [a fighter's term for a boxer who can't take a punch]. All you have to do to beat him is to walk into him and bang him with a solid punch. I don't think he'll ever whip another good fighter.[43]

Louis would prove Dempsey, and any others who doubted his ability, wrong.

The loss to Schmeling proved that Louis was indeed human and not a "jungle killer," as some racially prejudiced writers depicted him. Oddly, the loss earned considerable sympathy for Louis. It also instilled a new dedication and determination in Louis to become a world champion.

## The Comeback Trail

Louis began to realize what he meant to the black people of the nation and the world. "Here I was winning all the time and I lost one fight. During that time, when I was winning, I didn't understand how important I was to so many people."[44]

Louis recuperated from the damage Schmeling did to his face and his pride and began training again. His first fight would be against still another former heavyweight champion, Jack Sharkey. Sharkey held the title from 1932 to 1933 before he was dethroned by Schmeling. The Louis-Sharkey fight was set for August in New York.

By mid-July, just two months after the embarrassing loss to Schmeling, Louis was at the Pompton Lakes training camp where he had trained before. This time he listened intently to Chappie's instructions.

Sharkey was thirty-four, old for a boxer in those pre–George Foreman days, but he talked a great deal and said he would have no trouble with Louis. Chappie warned Joe that he (Sharkey) would pattern his fighting style after Schmeling's. After a cautious first round, Louis decked Sharkey in the second. Two more knockdowns came in the third round—one for a count of nine, and another for an eight count. Finally, Louis downed Sharkey for a third time in the third round. Sharkey stayed down for the count of ten, and Louis won by a knockout.

Louis thought he was ready for a rematch with Schmeling, but Max wanted to fight Jim Braddock, the reigning heavy-

*Louis and former heavyweight champion Jack Sharkey get in a tangle of jabs during Louis's first fight after his embarrassing loss to Schmeling.*

weight champion, for the title before fighting Louis again. Instead, Joe took on Al Ettore in Philadelphia on September 22 and knocked him out in the fifth round. On October 9, Louis kayoed Jorge Brescia in New York. Then came four very quick exhibition matches—all KOs for Louis.

So much for the exhibitions. On December 14, Louis would fight his last bout of 1936 in Cleveland against a solid boxer named Eddie Simms.

Sports historian Dr. Stan Grosshandler was a youngster living in Youngstown, Ohio, at the time. An uncle took him to Cleveland, about an hour away, for the fight. Grosshandler recalls:

> Check this out, but I think it was the fastest fight on record. It still may be [Louis's fight with Simms lasted 26 seconds—and it was a record until a 1946 fight in England lasted only 10.5 seconds]. The bell sounded to start the fight. Simms came out and threw one punch. It missed. Louis countered with a left that broke Simms's jaw. That quick, it was over![45]

In fairness to Simms, he was a last-minute substitute for Johnny Risko, who

*Louis regains some lost esteem when he finishes his fight with Jack Sharkey by knocking out the veteran boxer.*

## Propaganda Victory

*The Nazis used Max Schmeling's victory over Joe Louis to attest to the supposed superiority of white over black. In* Hitler's Games, *Duff Hart-Davis quotes a Nazi newspaper on Schmeling's victory.*

"It was more than a boxing match. Here black and white confronted each other, and all the foes of Nazi Germany, whatever their color, reckoned on the brutal overthrow of the German [Schmeling]. It was not only Joe Louis that was defeated. The sporting spirit of the great masses of population felt instinctively that our comrade saved the reputation of the white race.

Schmeling's victory was not only sport. It was a question of prestige for our race. With his hard fists he has won the respect of the world for the German nation—from which we shall conclude that we have only ourselves to rely upon, and that nobody presents us with anything for which we have not fought."

suffered broken ribs while training to fight Louis.

Joe would fight three times in early 1937, knocking out Steve Ketchel and Natie Brown, whom he also fought in 1935, and getting a ten-round decision in Madison Square Garden from Bob Pastor, who mostly stayed away from Louis and clinched when he did get close.

By this time, nearly everyone who followed boxing even on a casual basis knew that Joe Louis was something special. He was a devastating puncher, and his recent bouts proved it. He dispatched good fighters in record time and physically hurt some of them while doing so. Except for the single knockout by Schmeling, Louis's record as a professional fighter was unblemished.

Next up for Louis was what he and his many followers had been waiting for—a fight for the world title against heavyweight champion Jim Braddock.

Chapter

# 5 Joe Louis, World Champion

Joe Louis was at the lowest point in his boxing career after his defeat at the hands of Schmeling. He admitted this to himself and the public, but in the style of the true champion he was about to become, he did something about it. He learned from the humiliating experience. He worked hard and once again became a serious contender for the opportunity to fight a heavyweight title bout.

Originally, Louis's handlers—Roxborough, Black, and Mike Jacobs—tried to get a return bout with Schmeling, but Schmeling had a contract to fight Braddock for the championship.

Propaganda figured in the proposed match between Schmeling and Braddock. Many observers of the world political scene felt Schmeling was a "tool" of the Nazi Party. Since the Nazis believed Schmeling could beat Braddock, they wanted him only to fight Braddock and win the heavyweight title. If Schmeling took the title from Braddock, the thinking was, he would hurry back to Germany and either not fight at all or fight only boxers whom he knew he could beat.

Louis echoed this idea: "The talk was, he figured to take the championship back to Germany so the Nazi party could claim he won because he was one of the super race."[46]

## See You in Court

Mike Jacobs was intent on getting Louis a shot at the championship by fighting Jim Braddock, but Braddock and Max Schmeling had entered into an agreement with the Madison Square Garden promoters that they wouldn't fight any other matches before the fight for the heavyweight title. Jacobs, a man who knew most if not all the angles, looked at the contract between the fighters and Madison Square Garden. To be valid, a contract has to obligate both sides to perform a specified act. Jacobs thought this contract obligated the fighters, but not Madison Square Garden—it was a one-sided deal. The contract tied up Braddock, the champ, but didn't obligate the promoters. Jacobs took the matter to court, and a New Jersey judge ruled that Jacobs was right. On appeal, higher courts also agreed with Jacobs.

Jacobs then made a deal with Braddock and Braddock's promoters to fight Louis instead of Schmeling. The deal required some hard selling. To convince the Braddock group to fight Louis, Jacobs offered them 10 percent of his profits from any heavyweight fights that Jacobs would promote for the next ten years. The Braddock group was entitled to 10 percent of what Mike Jacobs earned from Louis's or any other heavyweight fights for the next decade. As it turned out, it was a good deal for both sides: Louis got a crack at the title, and Braddock had secured substantial future earnings no matter how his own boxing career went.

Once the Madison Square Garden–Schmeling–Braddock case was settled, Jacobs went to Chicago and met with a representative from the Illinois attorney general's office and the state athletic commission in order to have the fight officially sanctioned—a necessary step in all championship fights. Jacobs received the go-ahead for the fight. The contract was drawn up to have Louis meet Braddock on June 22, 1937, a Tuesday night, in Comiskey Park.

## The Training Grind

Not wanting to blow the opportunity he had worked, and reworked, so hard for, Louis took his training for the Braddock fight and the title shot very seriously. Camp was set up in Kenosha, Wisconsin, on Lake Michigan not far from Chicago. Louis and his party went into camp in mid-May. Louis remembered the effort to prepare for the fight:

> I worked harder for it than any fight I remember. Chappie got me up at five o'clock every morning for six weeks and I would run ten miles on the road, running when the sun was hardly up. I had a big string of sparring partners and I would work out with them. I would knock off around five o'clock in the evening, have supper, then go to bed around nine o'clock, and a full eight hours of sleep.[47]

The hard training paid off. Louis was sharp, and at the weigh-in, he scaled just what he and his trainers wanted him to—197¼ pounds. He was ready.

## Fighting for the Title

Normally, the challenger enters the ring first, so that the champion can make a later triumphant entrance. But on this night Braddock came into the ring first. He and Louis were waiting in the dressing room of the White Sox ballpark, but Braddock got impatient and went into the ring. Louis wasn't far behind. As the cheering for both boxers died down, other noted boxers such as former champions Jack Dempsey, Gene Tunney, and Barney Ross were introduced. Referee Tommy Thomas gave his instructions and the fight was about to begin.

As he sent Louis out to answer the opening bell, Chappie said to Louis, "This is it, Chappie. You come home a champ tonight."[48]

Louis hit Braddock pretty solidly in the first round, but did little apparent damage to the champ. Later Braddock landed a combination of punches and took the same from Louis. Then he took a left and a right from Louis, blocked a right, and threw a short right uppercut that knocked Louis off his feet. Louis bounced up before the referee hardly began his count. The two heavyweights continued to box each other for the rest of the round.

When Louis got to his corner after the round, Chappie scolded him for not staying down longer when Braddock took him off his feet. "Why didn't you take a nine-

*Jim Braddock endures a barrage of thunderous blows as Louis fights for the world champion title.*

count? You can't get up so fast that nobody in the place didn't see you was down."[49]

Louis really hurt Braddock in the second round, landing strong, stinging, solid combinations. Braddock gamely hung on and was probably saved by the bell at the end of the round. Louis sensed he had Braddock set for a finish, but Chappie Blackburn advised him to keep punching and getting out of the way. He reasoned that Braddock was experienced enough and game enough that if Louis made a mistake, the champ could still beat the young challenger. Louis did as he was told through the third, fourth, fifth, and sixth rounds.

By the seventh, it was evident that Chappie's strategy was a wise one. Braddock looked tired to everyone in Comiskey Park, including Louis. Louis landed most of the punches in the round. Braddock was not doing much more than clinching and staying out of harm's way as best he could. Louis felt that Braddock was about at the end of the line and was set to throw a hard right when the bell sounded, giving Braddock at least a few more minutes as heavyweight champion of the world. As Louis was still walking back to his corner, Braddock was already slumped on a stool in his corner with seconds (those who attend to a boxer in between rounds) working on him. At least one of Braddock's seconds wanted to throw in the towel, but the champion would hear none of it. He wanted to go down or go out fighting.

When Louis was a young fighter, Chappie told him to always watch his opponent's hands. A fresh boxer will hold his hands at a normal height to protect himself. A tired boxer, having to make an effort to get his hands up, will overcompensate and hold them too high. In the eighth, Braddock not only held his hands too high, he also threw punches that were weak and off target. Louis seemed to be able to hit Braddock any way and any time he wanted. Braddock missed a punchless right. Louis faked throwing a left and landed a lightninglike right to Braddock's head. Braddock doubled over, appeared to start back up, but then tumbled face first to the canvas. Referee Thomas, after pointing Joe to a neutral corner, began his count as the Comiskey Park crowd of forty-five thousand, nearly half of them black, screamed wildly in response to what they were seeing. After Braddock was officially counted out, at one minute, ten seconds in the round, and Louis's hand was raised in triumph, the world had a new heavyweight champion—and he was a black man. This victory marked only the second time that a black man held the most coveted sports title in the world.

Louis was just twenty-three, the youngest man to ever hold the most important trophy in all of sports.

## The Celebration

Louis seemed to be in a daze by what he had accomplished—from cotton picker to champion:

> I don't remember going back to the dressing room. I started feeling light inside my body, but it wasn't from any

*After taking a beating, Braddock is officially counted out, making Louis heavyweight champion of the world.*

blows I got in the ring. I never felt like this in my life. Chappie could see what was coming and pushed me to a rubbing table; I was about to faint. I guess everything came down on me then."[50]

The dressing room was filled with well-wishers: governors of many states, mayors of many large cities, socialites, movie stars, athletes from other sports. This was at a time when a heavyweight championship fight was the most important sporting event in the country. Few people were unaware of what was happening.

A tremendous crowd was waiting for Joe and Marva as they tried to leave the baseball stadium. Many blacks in the crowd shouted encouragement to Joe and left little doubt that they were counting on him to advance their cause.

Marva had arranged a small, mostly family gathering at their home, but before Joe joined in the celebration he telephoned his mother in Detroit to assure her that he was all right. She told him that hundreds of people were outside of her house and that they cheered loudly when she went out on the porch.

### New Champ on the Old Champ

*Joe Louis, writing in* Life *magazine in a lengthy article entitled "My Story," pays tribute to the gallant effort champion Jim Braddock made in the fight in which Louis became heavyweight champion of the world. Louis, like many true fight fans of the time, had great respect for the older Braddock.*

"Braddock carried the fight to me in the second, but I got in three hard ones. I rocked him good. It made him a little wild and he punched almost blind. I landed some hard ones in the third and saw him weaken some, but he hit me a bad body punch. I opened his lip and I got some more hard rights to his face, but he stood up to them. He's a tough fighter with a solid punch, that Braddock.

He stayed with me long after I figured he could. I tried to put him out in the fifth, the sixth, and the seventh, and he wobbled but kept coming at me and I couldn't put a finisher on him.

People figure that was my biggest thrill, beating Braddock for the title, but it was no different to me from winning any other fight. I don't remember any special feeling. I just felt good.

Maybe it was because I figured in my own mind I wouldn't feel like a real champ until I got that Schmeling. That's what I fixed on. After I got the title any man who wanted a shot at me, he could have it. That's what I figured to do if I got the title, and that's the way it was."

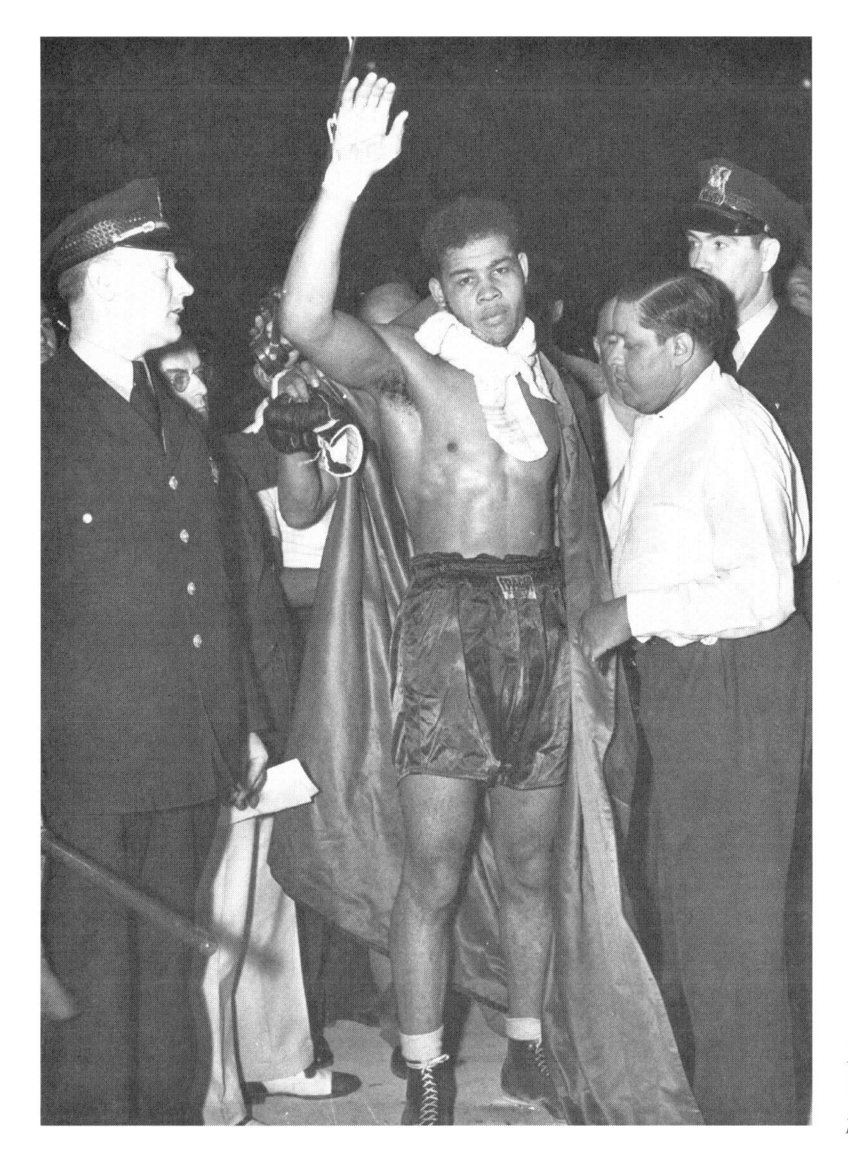

*Louis raises his hand in triumph shortly after he is pronounced world champion.*

The city of Chicago celebrated, too. Thousands stayed up all night, shouting and running through the streets. There was no intentional destruction, as has been the case with celebrations of sports victories in more recent years, just a feeling of joy and excitement.

Harlem, the black community on New York's upper Manhattan Island, also took to the streets after listening to Louis's triumph on the radio. A loosely constructed parade of thousands marched up Seventh Avenue and down Lennox Avenue most of the night.

The next day, Louis and his managers attended a press conference that Mike Jacobs held in Chicago's Morrison Hotel. Newsreels of the previous night's fight were shown, telegrams (a popular way of quick communication in those days) were read, and business opportunities presented. Louis recalled the moment:

> All kinds of offers were given to me, stage offers, movie offers, radio offers, offers to referee fights at $1,000 a match. About $500,000 was put up for grabs. And, just think, five years before I was happy to get those seven-dollar merchandise checks for an amateur fight.[51]

With his stepbrother Pat Brooks driving, Joe and Marva took off for Detroit. Brooks would remain Joe's driver until Joe retired from the ring. Roxborough and Black had barred Joe from driving after hearing reports that Joe and his old pal Freddie Guinyard were speeding around Chicago at ninety miles per hour. Also along for the trip was Carl Nelson, who would be part of Louis's entourage for many years. For want of a better term, Nelson—a large man—was often referred to as Louis's "bodyguard." In reality, he was a friend who helped keep overzealous fans away from Joe. Certainly, the new heavyweight champion did not need a bodyguard.

Joe's mother, with help from fellow church ladies, had a feast prepared for Joe. Although Joe and Marva sneaked into Detroit at night, word got out that the champ and his wife were in town and fans soon were hanging around his mother's

### A Gallant Old Champion

*Joe Louis captured the heavyweight championship in 1937 by defeating Jim Braddock. Braddock was old for a fighter; Louis was very young. In an article entitled "Joe Louis: Greatest of Champions," Jimmy Cannon paints a picture of a determined old champion—Braddock.*

"It was obvious that Braddock didn't have a chance. The people in his corner demanded that Jimmy quit. But Braddock said no and Louis took care of him and gave him a terrible beating. I was supposed to have filed a humorous story of the fight, but I asked them [his editors] to let me out of it because I could locate no comedy in the butchery of a guy who was brave according to the rules of his profession. I tell you this because Braddock was better than the record in the book. I doubt if Jimmy ever considered himself a valorous man, but he was when you compare him with some of those who made more money by running and holding. So you must take his opinion of Louis seriously and appraise the champion [Louis] by what he says.

'Nobody hits like Louis,' Braddock said.

'What about Max Baer?' I said.

'A joke compared to that Louis,' Braddock insisted."

house. Joe endured all the attention, as well as requests for money, which he usually granted. Then he left to go to Washington, D.C., to see his buddy John Henry Lewis fight. Lewis pleased Joe by defeating Willie Reddish.

If Louis had been like previous heavyweight champions, he could have taken an extended vacation from the ring and cashed in on fighting exhibitions and making personal appearances, such as the offers that were proposed at the postfight press conference. He chose not to follow that example. To illustrate how the old-timers treated their heavyweight crowns, it should be pointed out that from August of 1928 through June of 1937, there had been only seven heavyweight championship fights. Braddock held the title for two full years without defending it until his fight with Louis.

To be a fighting champion, something Roxborough and Black felt Louis had to be, Joe and Mike Jacobs signed a new five-year contract. It called for four title defenses a year. Joe was young enough to stand the pace, his spending habits required the constant income, and Jacobs would not get any money personally unless Louis fought.

Louis, and the world, wanted a rematch with Schmeling to give Louis a chance to remove the only blemish on his record as a professional fighter. Schmeling knew, or thought, he was in a strong bargaining position. He asked for 30 percent of the gate receipts instead of the challenger's normal 20 percent. Jacobs turned down the suggestion. Schmeling then planned to fight a Welsh coal miner, Tommy Farr, who was the champion of the British Isles. If he won, Schmeling could rightfully call himself the champion of Europe, and he reasoned, since he had beaten Louis, champion of the world.

But before Schmeling could get Farr to agree to a fight, Jacobs offered the British boxer sixty thousand dollars to fight Louis in New York. This represented about twice as much as Farr stood to make in a fight with Schmeling. He jumped at the chance, and the cash, and signed a contract to fight Louis in August.

## Fighting Farr

Farr proved to be as tough as his job of mining coal. He went the full fifteen rounds with Louis, but lost the decision and took a real physical beating. A photo in a little-noted and long-forgotten magazine, *Sports Stars*, shows Farr after the fight with a bandaged broken ring finger and deep cuts under both eyes, as well as other marks on his face.

Louis had a great deal of respect for Farr, though, saying:

> He stayed the fifteen rounds with me when the writers said he couldn't. I didn't play with Tommy Farr, like some thought, and I didn't cut him on purpose. I liked that Tommy Farr. He had guts. He just kept coming and I had to stop him.[52]

It wasn't too long after the Louis-Farr fight that Schmeling signed, at 20 percent, to fight Louis on June 22, 1938, a year away.

Chapter

# 6 Schmeling—Rematch and Retribution

It is hard to overestimate the importance of Louis's second fight with Max Schmeling. For many Americans at the time, and even citizens throughout the world, it was the defining moment in Louis's boxing career. Later generations could reflect back on this championship fight as Louis's "greatest moment" among many great moments and outstanding achievements.

Obviously, the rematch would be an opportunity for Louis to eradicate his humiliating defeat of 1936. The rematch would also vindicate the issues apparent in the first match: German, and especially Aryan, superiority and, by extension, black inferiority.

Thus a heavy responsibility rested on the broad shoulders of the heavyweight champion who had turned twenty-four years old the previous month. America adopted Joe as its standard-bearer, and people around the world who were opposed to the aggressive tactics of Nazi Germany placed their hopes on the same broad shoulders.

*Louis loved to golf and played as often as he could. He was so intent to win his second fight with Schmeling, however, that he abstained from the sport while training for the fight.*

## No Golf, Just Boxing

One measure of how seriously Louis was training for the Schmeling rematch was that he left his golf clubs at home. He had become devoted to the game and played as often as he could. Even in a normal training camp, known to be an all-business-little-pleasure experience, Louis played golf several times a week.

As Schmeling had attended several of Louis's workouts and his fight with Tommy Farr, Louis and Chappie Blackburn watched Schmeling fight Harry Thomas. They observed Schmeling's techniques carefully and set up a training routine to prepare Louis for the Schmeling rematch. Louis remembered, "I went to Pompton Lakes [the New Jersey training camp] sure that I had him [Schmeling] figured out, and Chappie put my sparring partners to throwing hard rights at me. I got so I could block them easy."[53]

Louis trained rigorously and seriously for the fight. He admitted to himself and the public that he was overconfident in the 1936 bout with Schmeling. This complacency would not happen again, and leaving the golf clubs home to gather dust was just a small token of Louis's seriousness.

## The Champion and the President

Rumors had it that even the president wanted Louis to understand the importance of the fight to world politics. When Louis was in Washington, D.C., President Roosevelt invited him to the White House.

Louis recounted the occasion:

> Mr. Roosevelt sent his car for me. A man took us [he had an old friend Mal Frazier go with him] into the President's office. The President [who was confined to a wheelchair because of polio] had me lean over so he could feel my muscles. He said, "Joe, we need muscles like yours to beat Germany." That's the only thing he said.[54]

President Roosevelt reportedly told Louis that millions of people were counting on him to deal Schmeling and Hitler an embarrassing defeat. However, the president, if he indeed had said so, wouldn't have been so specific. Joe was determined enough to win for his own personal satisfaction. Any outside motivation was unnecessary.

In *Sport* magazine, Jack Sher describes the White House visit in more detail: "They chatted for a few minutes. 'Joe,' the President said, 'when the cause is right, an American never loses.' 'I won't let you down, Mr. President,' Joe replied."[55]

It seemed incongruous that the president of the United States (and a New York aristocrat) would appoint the son of Alabama sharecroppers as the standard-bearer of the United States and much of the free world. But the visit to the White House was an example of the stature Joe Louis was gaining in the public eye.

Louis's attitude going into the fight was one of angry revenge. Usually, Louis was concerned that he might hurt another fighter. He would often visit the dressing room of a boxer he had just knocked out to make sure his opponent was recovering in a satisfactory way. But Schmeling was different.

An account in the *New York Daily Mirror* by Murray Lewis quoted Louis as saying, "I'm out for revenge. All I ask of Schmeling is that he stand up and fight without quitting. I've waited two years for this chance and now my time has come."[56]

The *New York Times* quoted Roxborough:

> Ordinarily, Joe doesn't care who the other fellow is. It's just another fight for Joe. But this Schmeling, well, it's

*The weighing ceremony before the Louis-Schmeling rematch, a fight that captured the attention of people around the world.*

sorta got under Joe's skin. This time it isn't just another fighter; it's a chance to catch up to Schmeling and square an account.[57]

## Round One—and Done

Jacobs and Louis wisely chose the location for the second Schmeling fight. To take advantage of the tremendous prefight interest, the rematch was planned for Yankee Stadium, perhaps the most prestigious outside locale and one that could accommodate the anticipated crowd of seventy-thousand on June 22, 1937.

> I took a long warm-up in my dressing room. When I climbed into the ring I was in a light sweat, the way I like to be for a fight. Me and Chappie talked about what I was going to do, and I just went out. I knew I was going to take Max Schmeling that night.

Schmeling threw the first punch. It was a right and missed. A good omen for Louis. Louis led with a hard left jab, and Schmeling dropped his guard. Louis shot a right to Schmeling's jaw. He said, "I put my body into it. I put my heart into it. I threw him on the ropes and his knees buckled."[58]

Louis continued to hammer away. It was still the first round. Referee Arthur Donovan wrote in his daily journal:

> Schmeling tried to counter the fusillade [flurry of punches] of ripping rights and lefts. Louis ignored it. Louis smashed home another right that could have dented concrete. . . . Schmeling had no chance. Schmeling crumpled for keeps. That was the end of the massacre.[59]

The punch that Louis threw, the one that Donovan said could have dented concrete, was not without controversy. It landed in the area of Schmeling's kidney.

Few who saw it, or later viewed it on film, thought it was unsportsmanlike. Joe was pounding Max almost at will. As Louis started the powerhouse right, Schmeling turned to avoid the punch and unwittingly exposed the area of his kidney. Only in Germany, or wherever there were Nazi sympathizers, was the blow termed "dirty." It landed in a vulnerable place, but it was Schmeling who left himself open to the blow.

Sportswriter Jack Sher further commented, "Joe Louis hit Max Schmeling forty-one times on that night. He hit him most of those times with the right hand that Max had held in contempt."[60]

Jimmy Cannon, a widely read columnist, later said, "If ever a fighter made a perfect fight, Joe did that night."[61]

The fight with the two-year buildup was over in two minutes and four seconds. Louis was simply overwhelming. Whether Schmeling knew it or not coming into the fight, he never had a chance.

The two brief minutes it took Louis to defeat Schmeling captured nearly all that made Joe Louis a great champion.

Louis was in a position few will ever find themselves in; a single event that decides whether one's life's work is a success or a failure, with no second chance and much of the world watching. Louis was

*Louis's powerful punch lands Schmeling on the ropes.*

able to summon his courage, self-control, and talent to perform as a hero.

## Celebrations

The victory over Schmeling was celebrated throughout the nation. The black community of Harlem celebrated long into the night with parades and parties. People poured into the streets to talk about the fight. The scene was very similar to the celebration that had taken place when Louis defeated Braddock for the world championship. Louis was part of it. He recalled, "I went out with Marva in Harlem and we had a real party. My pay for the second Schmeling fight was $135,000."[62]

In his acclaimed memoir *Growing Up*, Russell Baker, the noted *New York Times* columnist, recounted what it was like to live on Baltimore's Lombard Street, in an integrated section of the city, when Louis scored his lightning-quick knockout over Schmeling. Baltimore was a "southern city," and racial prejudice existed. So did a belief in "white supremacy."

*An ecstatic Harlem crowd celebrates Louis's lightning-quick defeat of Schmeling.*

### A Referee's Perspective

*Arthur Donovan was a well-known boxing official. He refereed many of Joe Louis's championship fights. His son Art Jr. became a Pro Football Hall of Famer after playing for the Baltimore Colts. The younger Donovan included an entry from his father's journal in the book* Fatso, *Art Jr.'s autobiography.*

"Louis came out, making a winding motion with his right forearm—the very same gesture with which he had come to the ring center for his first battle with the German [in 1936].

'Hasn't he learned anything from that one?' I asked myself.

In twelve seconds Louis answered with a jolt to Schmeling's jaw that staggered the German. Then another, and another, and another. There was no dropped guard after the hitting.

'He's learned all he needed to know,' I said to myself.

A vicious right to the kidneys and Schmeling screamed in pain—the most terrifying sound I ever heard in a ring. I stepped between them just as Louis poised another bomb.

'Get away, Joe,' I said.

He blinked and backed away, cold eyes boring in on the German.

I knew I couldn't be wrong stopping the fight. Schmeling crumpled for keeps, and I breast-stroked with both arms to keep Louis away. That was the end of the massacre. Max went to the hospital with polysyllabic fractures. I don't like to speculate where he'd have gone had Louis struck another lightning bolt."

Baker recalled how the whites living on Lombard Street never showed much outward interest in Louis's career and that the blacks who lived in the alley (Lemmon Street) behind Lombard "thought too much celebration would be indiscreet."[63]

Things changed for Baker and the neighborhood in the months leading up to the Louis-Schmeling rematch. As was the case in most of America, blacks and whites were preoccupied with the scope of the fight. Blacks saw Louis as "their" fighter. Whites saw Louis as either a black fighter, whom they didn't necessarily want to defeat a white boxer, or as a man who could strike a blow against Nazism by defeating a German boxer.

Baker maintains that the majority of whites, regardless of their feelings toward Hitler and the Nazis, still wanted Schmeling to win. To them, whatever else Schmeling was, he was primarily a white man

### "Some Black Mother's Son"

*Writing in* I Know Why the Caged Bird Sings, *poet and writer Maya Angelou tells of the shared joy of Joe Louis's world championship.*

"Then the voice, husky and familiar, came to wash over us—'The winnah, and champeen of the world . . . Joe Louis.'

Champion of the world. A Black boy. Some Black mother's son. He was the strongest man in the world. People drank Coca-Colas like ambrosia and ate candy bars like Christmas. Some of the men went behind the store and poured white lightning [a clear home-distilled whiskey] in their softdrink bottles, and a few of the bigger boys followed them. Those who were not chased away came back blowing their breath in front of themselves like proud smokers.

It would take more than an hour before the people would leave the store and head for home. Those who lived too far had made arrangements to stay in town. It wouldn't do for a Black man and his family to be caught on a lonely country road on a night when Joe Louis proved that we were the strongest people in the world."

fighting a black man, and their support would be with the white man no matter what the government of his country was doing to the people of Europe. While still a few years before the United States entered World War II, the world was aware of Hitler's threats to blacks, Jews, and other minorities and his annexation of peaceful nations. In this instance, Hitler's threat didn't seem to matter that much.

Baker continues his remembrance by describing the scene after the fight:

> From Lemmon Street I heard the customary whooping and cheering rise from the sour Baltimore night. I went to the kitchen window. Doors were being flung open down there [Lemmon Street]. People were streaming out into the alley, pounding each other delightedly on the back, roaring with exultation. Then I saw someone start to move up the alley, out toward white territory, and the rest of the group, seized by an instinct to defy destiny, falling in behind him and moving en masse.
>
> I watched them march out of the alley and turn the corner, then ran to the front of the apartment to see if they were coming into Lombard Street. They were. They seemed to have been joined by other groups pouring out of other neighborhood alleys for there was a large throng now coming

around into Lombard Street, marching right out in the middle of the street as though it was their street, too. Men in shirt-sleeves, women, boys and girls, mothers carrying babies—they moved down Lombard Street almost silently except for a low murmur of conversation and an occasional laugh. Nervous laughter, most likely.

Joe Louis had given them the courage to assert their right to use a public thoroughfare, and there wasn't a white person down there to dispute it. It was the first civil rights demonstration I ever saw, and it was completely spontaneous, ignited by the finality with which Joe Louis had destroyed the theory of white superiority. The march lasted maybe five minutes, only as long as it took the entire throng to move slowly down the full length of the block. Then they turned the corner and went back into the alleys and, I guess, felt better than most of them had felt for a long time.[64]

Baker's anecdote recalls what Louis came to symbolize for other blacks. He was truly a symbol of hope and a source of pride to blacks throughout the nation.

## Meanwhile Back in Germany

When it became obvious that Louis was pounding Schmeling into submission, German authorities cut off the shortwave radio broadcast to the German people. The German government prohibited the showing of films of the fight. The Nazis did not want the German people to see their "champion" humiliated by a black American.

While the German propaganda machine was quick to call Schmeling's first victory "a national triumph," it was equally

*Schmeling reveals his battered face—which was exposed to only two minutes of Louis's attack—to talk with the public after his fall in the ring.*

## Schmeling II

*Probably no fight in boxing history was more dramatic than the rematch between Joe Louis and Max Schmeling, the only man—up to that time—to defeat Louis professionally. In* The Pictorial History of Boxing, *Nat Fleischer and Sam Andre vividly describe Louis's great victory.*

"The fists of the Bomber [Louis] crushed his former conqueror in a manner that left no doubt about his [Louis's] superiority. Though Schmeling complained bitterly about being struck foul kidney punches, every blow was a fair one. Any that struck Max in the kidneys were caused by the twisting of Schmeling's body as he held on to the upper strand of ring ropes and tried desperately to avoid the vicious attack of his opponent.

The first knockdown followed a right to the chin. The German fell on his shoulder and rolled over twice before coming to rest with his feet in the air. Max was down twice more. The second time, after a count of two, he got to his feet, a powerful right crashed against his jaw and Max went down on all fours. He tried to straighten himself to rise, but while in the process, his chief second, Max Machon, tossed the towel in the ring. Since this was not permitted under New York rules, referee Arthur Donovan hurled it back out, took a good look at Schmeling, and as the timekeeper reached the count of eight, Donovan halted the bout.

The King [Louis] had proved his right to the throne."

*Schmeling desperately tries to protect himself against Louis's devastating blows.*

quick to lessen the importance of Schmeling's loss in the second fight. Chris Mead quotes Arno Hellmis in a German publication, "One thing has to be said quite clearly. The defeat of a boxer does not mean any loss of national prestige."[65] Another publication said, "It is bitter, but it is not a national disaster."[66]

Germany sent its ambassador to America to visit Schmeling in the hospital, where he was taken after the fight. The ambassador asked Schmeling to file a protest over the foul blow, but Schmeling assured the diplomat that nothing illegal had taken place.

Despite the assurances of the German boxer through his nation's ambassador, *Der Arbeitsmann*, a publication of the Nazi Labor Corps (a German trade union), explained incorrectly and outrageously that "the American [Louis] was a wild monster of the jungle, who knows how to beat white men by a barrage of cheating blows to the liver."[67]

Regardless of excuses and accusations coming out of Germany, the vast majority of the people of all nations were happy with Louis's victory.

## The Fruits of Victory

After the decisive victory over Schmeling, Louis did not fight again in 1938. He took time off from training and boxing. Louis earlier put together the Brown Bombers softball team and went on the road for a while with them. Louis and his old neighborhood buddies from East Detroit traveled first class in big buses, stayed in top-rated hotels, and ate good meals. The season, with Louis picking up all the bills, cost him about fifty thousand. In addition to financing his ball team, Louis shared his wealth with relatives, down-and-out friends, old fighters, strangers, and favorite charities.

Cars were something else on which Louis spent money. He bought a Buick Roadmaster for his mother, a car for Marva, and a car for his sister Vunies. Louis was also very proud of sending Vunies to college. She was enrolled at Howard University (and would graduate in 1940, teach English in Detroit, and later earn a master's degree in history).

Louis also bought houses in Detroit for members of the Barrow-Brooks family, an apartment house in Chicago that he and Marva managed, and a horse farm outside of Utica, Michigan. Most were sound investments, but Louis would lose money backing a nightclub and a fried chicken restaurant. However, life for the young champion seemed to be going well.

One of the charities Louis supported was Detroit's Phyllis Wheatley Home for Old Ladies. Louis gave a considerable sum to the home and clearly delighted in the affection he received from its residents. He said:

> I give them some money every year. When I go out there they talk about boxing. Mr. Roxborough got them a radio-phonograph and they tune in every time I'm in the ring. They all call me "son." That gives me around twenty mothers.[68]

Chapter

# 7 Taking On All Comers

The life of a champion may have seemed like the good life. In some respects it was, especially for Joe. But the constant demands on his time, whether boxing or just making appearances, took its toll on Marva. She was not cut out for the nonstop travel and did not always accompany Joe. Sometimes it was impossible for her to join him; other times she chose to stay home. During these times away from Marva, Joe would stray. Plenty of women wanted to enjoy the company of the heavyweight champion of the world, and Joe showed little resistance to the temptations of the road. He had affairs, neglected Marva, and generally damaged their marriage to the point that it would never be fully repaired.

*In Paris in 1948, beauty pageant contestants gather around Louis, who showed little resistance to flirtatious female fans.*

The lifestyle of the champion bothered Marva so much that she once felt compelled to visit the famous Mayo Clinic in Rochester, Minnesota, after she suffered a miscarriage. Doctors there told Joe and his managers that Marva was about to have a nervous breakdown unless Joe could offer a more consistent lifestyle and spend more time with her.

## Back at the Ranch

After this incident, Joe spent more time with Marva at Spring Hill, the horse farm outside of Detroit. He used Spring Hill as

## A Plea for Help

*Perhaps no one in modern history meant as much to black Americans as civil rights leader Dr. Martin Luther King Jr. In his 1964 book,* Why We Can't Wait, *King told of a condemned man calling out for Joe Louis to save him from the gas chamber.*

"More than twenty-five years ago, one of the southern states adopted a new method of capital punishment. Poison gas supplanted the gallows. In its earliest stages, a microphone was placed inside the sealed death chamber. The first victim was a young Negro. As the pellet dropped into the container, and gas curled upward, through the microphone came these words: 'Save me, Joe Louis. Save me, Joe Louis. Save me, Joe Louis . . . .' It is heartbreaking enough to ponder the last words of any person dying by force. It is even more poignant to contemplate the words of this boy because they reveal the helplessness, the loneliness, and the profound despair of Negroes in that period."

a place to do some of his training for boxing and a place to "rough it" before actually going into a training camp.

With a riding academy also on the grounds of the ranch, Marva became an expert horsewoman and entered many riding shows in the area. Joe, from his days riding mules in the red clay country of Alabama, was always at home around animals and enjoyed riding the many horses at Spring Hill. But as heavyweight champion of the world, he needed to fight—to defend his crown.

After avenging the only defeat of his professional career by winning the rematch with Schmeling and taking some well-deserved time off from boxing, Joe was determined to be a fighting champion. Although he held the world championship for a year before fighting Schmeling a second time, Louis did not then think of himself as truly the heavyweight champion of the world. His victory over Schmeling, especially as decisive as it was, changed that perception. He would not rest on his laurels as previous heavyweight champs had done. He would fight anyone and everyone.

## Back Home Again

After defeating Bob Pastor, one of the many heavyweights Louis would fight from 1939 until he went into the service in World War II, Joe headed back to Spring Hill for relaxation and to spend more time with Marva.

While in residence at the ranch, Louis and Marva participated in horse shows. Louis even won prizes for his riding. These shows were similar to a horse show he helped initiate earlier, the first United

*Even after his decisive victory over Schmeling, Louis continued to fight—and beat—anyone and everyone. Here, Louis pummels heavyweight opponent Bob Pastor.*

States Negro Horse Show at the Utica Riding Club, which was very close to Spring Hill. At that show, Louis took a third place in fine-gaited saddle horse competition.

Louis enjoyed the spirit of competition and participation, recalling, "They were exciting affairs. And the big time sports people from everywhere came to them."[69]

Joe and Marva also took a vacation to Cuba. He remembered the adulation of the Cuban people:

> The crowd was even more enthusiastic about me than in America. I never knew so many black people were anywhere, except in Africa and America. The president, Fulgencio Batista [who would be overthrown by Fidel Castro twenty years later] greeted us. There we saw the luxury side, the dark-skinned Cubans we saw looked like they were doing better than a lot of blacks back home. We stayed at the El President Hotel, real fancy. Marva and I were getting on real well then.[70]

The harmony in the marriage was short-lived. When Joe and Marva got back to Detroit, singer Lena Horne was in town with the Charlie Barnett band, one of the better-known swing bands of the era. Louis's relationship with Horne began in Hollywood when he and Marva were there to make a movie following the match with Braddock when Louis won the heavyweight crown. Louis tried to avoid Horne by not going to the theater where she was performing, but eventually they met at a party. Joe had little resistance, and soon he and Horne were planning times and places where they could meet. While Joe's public image was one of devoted, though somewhat absent, husband, Lena Horne was not the first, last, nor only beautiful woman who enjoyed Joe's companionship. These continuous flirtations would destroy Joe's marriage.

## Title on the Line

After Joe took some time off, he climbed back into the ring and risked his title often—no less than four times in 1940.

With war raging in Europe, Louis continued to fight frequently—more frequently than any other heavyweight champion on record—and well. He fought nine times in 1941, risking his championship seven times and fighting two exhibition bouts. He won every fight. Sportswriters referred to the opponents in this phase of Louis's boxing career as the Bum of the Month Club, taking into account the frequency of the fights and, in their opinion, the caliber of the competition.

Jack Sher, writing in *Sport* magazine, put the so-called Bum of the Month Club in perspective. The fighters termed "bums" were mainly very good fighters. The best the world had to offer at the time. They just didn't measure up to Joe Louis as boxers, but then few fighters did at any other time either. Said Sher, "Most of the challengers were capable heavyweights, but not in the same class with Louis as boxers and punchers."[71]

Sher further explained why people came to see fights, to listen to them, and to read about them when they were pretty sure of the outcome: "Joe became such a symbol of the word 'champion' that people paid not to see whether he would win or lose—they knew he would win—but just to see Joe Louis."[72]

Ray Arcel, a longtime fight trainer, handled fourteen of Louis's opponents. He had to help carry so many of them out of the ring after Louis knocked them out, he became known as "the Meat Wagon."

One of Louis's 1941 opponents was anything but a bum. In June, Louis fought Billy Conn, the light heavyweight champion of the world, who recently vacated

*Louis joins Lena Horne in song at a Chicago nightclub in 1949. His relationship with Horne fueled discord in Louis's already troubled marriage.*

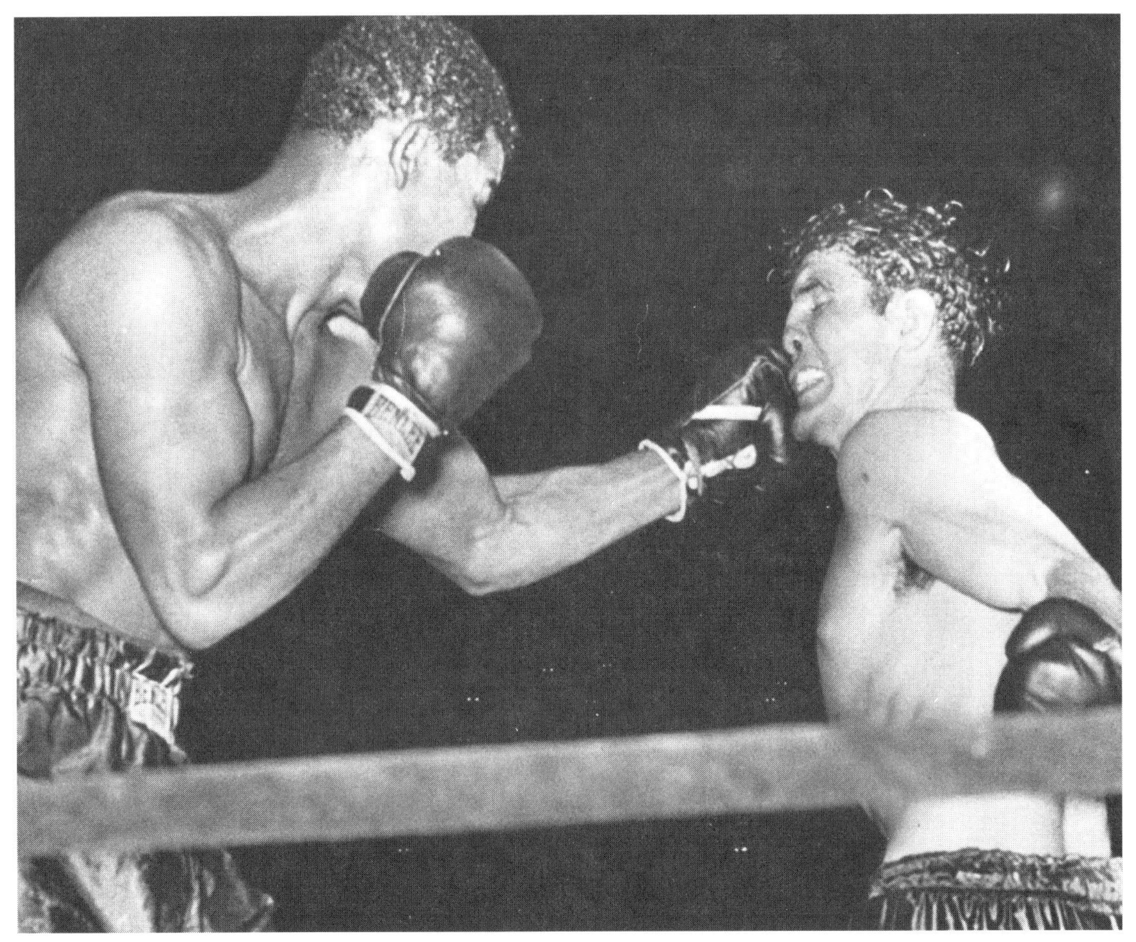

*Billy Conn reels in the wake of Louis's thunderous punch.*

his title and moved up a weight division to the heavyweight ranks. Because Conn, a likable Irishman from Pittsburgh, was a lighter fighter (175 pounds), Louis was determined to weigh in for the fight at less than 200 pounds. Despite weighing 60 pounds less than opponents such as Primo Carnera and Max Baer, Louis was sensitive to how it would look for a much bigger champion to be taking on a smaller challenger. He tipped the scales at the weigh-in at 199 pounds. Conn was lightning fast with his hands and was clearly giving Louis all he could handle in the early rounds. Fight fans watched in disbelief as Conn carried the fight to Louis. Then they became caught up in the excitement of the moment and actually cheered for Conn to win. At the end of the twelfth round, Chappie Blackburn told Louis, "You're losing on points. You gotta knock him out."[73]

In the thirteenth round, Conn was far ahead. All he needed to do to become the new heavyweight champion of the world was to successfully stay away from Louis's thunderous punches for this and another two rounds. But Conn did what he would admit later was a very foolish thing. He went for a knockout himself. He tried to stand up to Louis and slug it out with the champion, trading punch for punch.

Louis recounted the late stages of Conn's unlucky thirteenth round:

> He started that long left hook I'd been waiting for. I zapped a right to his head. He turned numb. Then I went into my routine of rights and lefts, rights and lefts. He went down. I saw him trying to get up, but he couldn't. Referee Eddie Joseph counted him out at two-minutes and fifty-eight seconds of the round.[74]

Once, years after the fight, when Louis and Conn met, Conn told Louis that he wished Joe would have let him have the title for just a while. Louis remarked with characteristic humor and truth, "I reckon, Billy, you had it for twelve rounds and didn't know what to do with it."[75]

While Louis was fighting nearly every month in 1941, he received a tremendous shock in April. Marva had filed for divorce, and the champion was caught off

**Singin' the Blues**

*Since the earliest days of the nation, Americans have written and sung about their folk heroes. To black America, Joe Louis was truly a folk hero. Many black musicians, through uniquely black music—the blues—wrote and sang songs about Louis. Chris Mead, in* Champion, *describes some of them.*

"Louis's victories over Carnera and Baer in 1935 inspired a host of songs. Though the black artists were blues singers, the songs differed from traditional blues in subject matter and mood. The early songs about Louis were exultant and happy, and in their portrayal of Louis as a heroic figure they resembled old Negro ballads. Memphis Minnie McCoy, with Black Bob at the piano, recorded 'He's in the Ring (Doin' the Same Old Thing),' and she also did the 'Joe Louis Strut.' Ike Smith recorded 'Fighting Joe Louis.' George Washington did 'Joe Louis Chant,' and Lil Johnson did 'Winner Joe (the Knock-Out King).' All these songs came out within a year after Louis broke into the big time with his knockout of Carnera in 1935. Billy Hicks and the Sizzling Six did 'Joe the Bomber' after he won the heavyweight championship in 1937, and Bill Gaither recorded a song about Louis's victory over Max Schmeling in their 1938 rematch.

The impression Joe Louis made on black music and oral culture only begins to suggest the depth of Louis's penetration into black consciousness in the 1930s."

guard. Marva explained to Joe that she wanted a husband who was around more, she wanted children, and she wanted a home that did not have a bunch of Joe's friends always hanging around. Joe knew Marva was right; they spent very little time together. If he wasn't in training camp, he was traveling to accept a special award. He was also chronically unfaithful. Louis pleaded his case "like a Supreme Court judge,"[76] and Marva dropped the proceedings, but eventually she filed for and was granted a divorce.

## America Goes to War

Like all young American men, Joe Louis had registered for the military draft—in his case, at his local draft board in Chicago in June 1940. His draft board had classified him 1-A, a rating that would make him eligible to be one of the first called into military service. Although the war in Europe was well under way, no one, including Louis, had expected the attack on the United States that came on December 7, 1941, when Japan bombed Pearl Harbor.

Louis could have claimed a deferment from active duty as the sole support of his mother, wife, and several brothers and sisters. But Louis had stated on a national radio network in mid-1941 that he was ready to go anytime Uncle Sam called him. He would repeat the statement several times between then and December 7.

Louis truly felt an obligation to serve his country, even if service meant giving up a rather comfortable lifestyle. Although he felt very patriotic, it is doubtful that Louis or anyone else realized what military service would mean to the heavyweight champion in terms of potential income lost. Another factor to be considered, but one for which there was no known outcome, was just how long Louis would be away from the ring and what effect the absence would have on his boxing. As it turned out, Louis lost several years from the prime of his career to World War II. But other Americans, in other careers, could make the same statement. Although more than fifty years have passed since the end of the war, it is hard to overestimate the turmoil that the global conflict brought to the lives of nearly everyone in the country.

Chapter

# 8 Private Joe Louis, U.S. Army

In the late 1930s and early 1940s, Joe Louis was a tremendous influence both on how black Americans viewed themselves and on how white Americans viewed blacks, but Louis exerted his most far-reaching influence as a soldier in uniform. He was instrumental in making changes in military policy, and, thus, in civil rights.

Without fanfare or flamboyance, Joe Louis made the black serviceman's lot a better one during World War II. At the same time, he contributed greatly to the war effort, both in a financial way and as a morale builder to the troops.

## Doing His Part

The entire country was swept up in a tidal wave of patriotism. Men by the thousands waited in line at enlistment centers to join the various branches of the military. Factories switched to making products needed for the war effort as quickly as possible. Everyone wanted to help; everyone was willing to sacrifice.

Mike Jacobs, like Louis, felt a sense of patriotism and sincerely wanted to help his country. Jacobs thought that Joe should donate the proceeds of a fight to war relief and asked the champ if he would be willing to risk his championship without receiving a purse (income) from the fight. Louis answered yes without hesitation. Jacobs arranged a fight between Louis and Buddy Baer. Baer was a giant of a man—six feet, six inches and 260 pounds. Louis at the time stood six feet, one inch and fought at about 200 pounds. Baer had fought Louis earlier in 1941 and with a powerful, if lucky, punch actually knocked Louis through the ropes and out of the ring. Louis recovered and won the bout when Baer was disqualified in the seventh round.

The rematch was set for January 9, 1942. The charity that would benefit was the Navy Relief Society, an organization set up to help the families of servicemen killed in the attack on Pearl Harbor a month earlier.

As Louis had done with others who defeated him or gave him unexpectedly hard fights, he vindicated himself in a return bout. Louis dispatched his larger opponent in the first round with two knockdowns before he decked Baer a third time and the referee counted him out.

When a writer suggested, after Louis donated his purse of fifty thousand dollars to Navy Relief, that Louis was fighting for nothing, Joe replied, "I ain't fighting for nothing; I'm fighting for my country." Louis possessed a knack for saying the

*Louis decks Buddy Baer in the early moments of their fight. Louis brought the much larger Baer down three times in the first round.*

right thing at the right time, and in the right way. The statement about fighting for his country only added to the praise and admiration he got from the public.

While others in the public eye, athletes and entertainers, did their part for America, it's doubtful that anyone risked more than Louis. He not only donated his fight purse but also risked losing the title, a title that was worth at least a million dollars to him. In addition, because of the speed with which the fight was arranged, Louis had to train quickly for the bout.

What Louis was doing was not lost on the public.

Burris Jenkins Jr., a sports cartoonist, drew a cartoon on the eve of the Louis-Baer fight with Uncle Sam holding Louis's right hand aloft in the traditional boxing sign of victory, and beneath the picture, Jenkins wrote, "In the most magnificent gesture ever made by a champion—to sacrifice not only his $50,000 winnings to Navy Relief, but to risk a million-dollar title—Joe Louis tonight can't fail to win the most priceless prize ever won in the world of sports." The prize was in the headline over the cartoon, "The Undying Admiration of His Countrymen."[77]

## Not Everyone Is Pleased

Although most Americans applauded Louis's patriotism, a few black journalists questioned Joe's choice of the Navy Relief Society as the beneficiary of his largesse. At the time, the U.S. Navy admitted relatively few blacks, and those who were allowed to enlist were given very menial jobs, such as cook and food server. Black sailors had no hope of becoming officers or serving in combat roles.

> The black *Pittsburgh Courier* pressed Louis to make a statement about discrimination in the navy before the fight, but Louis refused. Louis felt that if he quietly went ahead with the fight, he would do more to embarrass the navy and win over public opinion.[78]

## A Favor for a Favor

Right before Louis and Baer were getting ready to climb into the ring, Chappie Blackburn told Joe that his heart was bothering him a lot and he didn't think he could make it up to the ring and be in Louis's corner for the fight. Louis, who counted heavily on Blackburn's advice during a fight, would have been hampered seriously without Chappie. Although Louis certainly had the necessary skills and the confidence, he had grown very close to Chappie and depended on his friend.

Louis's response to Chappie was "You got to. If you get up those stairs with me, I'll have Baer out before you can even relax."[79]

Blackburn made it to the ring. But before the fight started, the Madison Square Garden crowd of seventeen thousand—and Blackburn—had to wait while military and civilian dignitaries were introduced in the flag-draped arena. One of those was 1940 presidential candidate Wendell Willkie, who said:

> Joe Louee [he always pronounced Louis's name as if it were French], your magnificent example of risking your title prompts us to say, "We thank you," and in view of your attitude it is impossible for me to see how any American can think of discrimination in terms of race, creed, or color.[80]

For his charitable fight to benefit Navy Relief, Joe was presented the Boxing Writers Association of New York's Edward J. Neil Award, named after a journalist who was killed while covering the Spanish Civil War and given to the man "who had done the most to project a positive image for boxing" the previous year.

At the dinner where Louis received the Neil Award, former New York mayor Jimmy Walker said of Louis's fight for Navy Relief, "You took your title and your future and bet it all on patriotism and love of country. Joe Louis, that night you laid a rose on the grave of Abraham Lincoln."[81] This statement was a reference to Lincoln's Emancipation Proclamation.

It was also at this dinner that Louis proved that his lack of formal education didn't prevent him from saying exactly what his eager public wanted to hear. When called upon for impromptu remarks, Joe said, "We gonna do our part, and we will win, because we are on God's side."[82] It was just what the crowd wanted to hear from the heavyweight champ, and they responded with a standing ovation of several minutes.

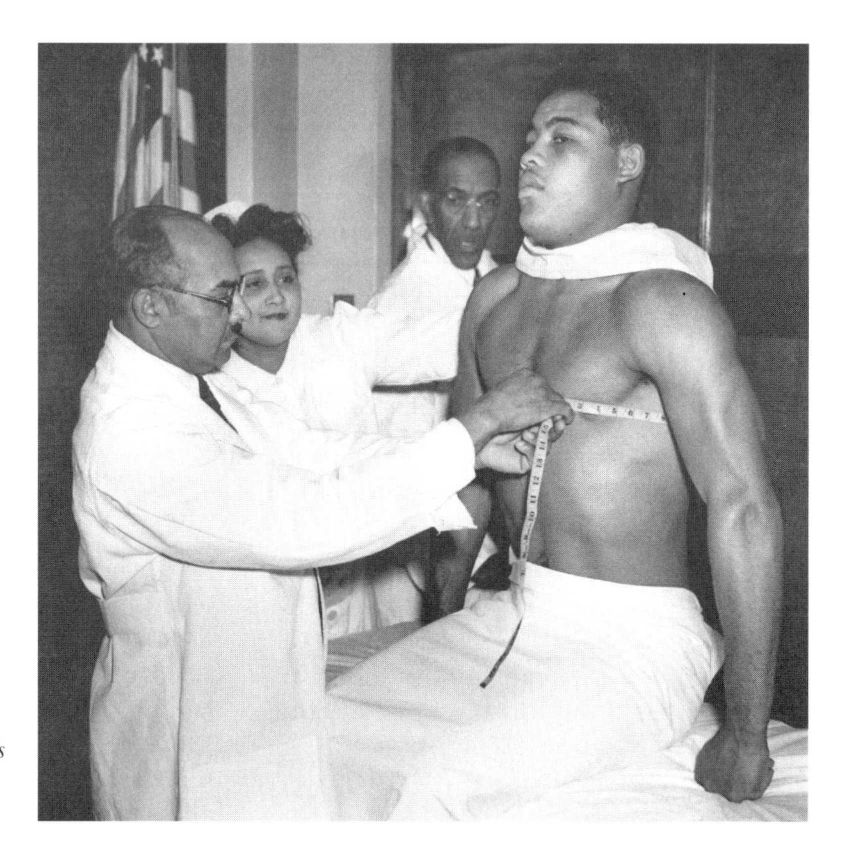

*Louis made headline news when he joined the army. Pictures like this one—Louis's army physical—appeared in newspapers coast to coast.*

## "You're in the Army Now"

After the glory of his last bout, Joe Louis joined the army. "You're in the Army Now" was a popular song at the start of World War II. It contrasted life as a civilian with that of a serviceman. Louis was among those who experienced the largest contrast in daily routines. Pictures of Louis expanding his chest, while an army doctor measured it at Governors Island (a military base in New York City) during his army physical appeared in newspapers coast to coast. A horde of writers and press photographers followed him to the physical examination.

An even bigger corps of media personnel tagged along when Louis reported to Camp Upton on Long Island the following day. With the nation at war for about a month, the media felt a patriotic duty to join with the War Department in publicizing the induction ceremonies of well-known Americans. The symbolism of America's heroes going off to war would have a profound effect on many average Americans. Enlistments were very high in the early days of the war.

Since becoming a title contender in 1935, Joe Louis was the only black to appear in the predominantly white national media on a consistent basis.

To whites, Joe Louis was the symbol of his race. Louis's generosity, his willingness to serve, and his patriotism assured whites about the loyalty of all black Americans. To a country deeply divided along racial

## A Quiet Influence

*While serving in the military, Joe Louis may have exerted more influence in the civil rights cause than at any other time. In an article in* Sport *magazine entitled "Brown Bomber, the Story of the Champ," Jack Sher describes Joe's relationship with his commanding officer and the troops.*

"Lou Krem, Joe's commanding officer in the army, likes to tell stories about Joe's influence on all kinds of people. Louis once visited a stockade full of prisoners, American soldiers in the guardhouse [a prisonlike building] for misconduct.

'When Joe walked into that big roomful of men,' Krem said, 'you could have heard a pin drop. Then he began to talk to them in that slow, deliberate way he has. I've never heard a speech like that. He told them that their uniforms weren't the one the army had given them. He said, as a soldier, he was ashamed of them [now in their prison uniforms]. Then he told them about a mistake he had made. He said he had thought he was a big shot before the first Schmeling fight. He said he forgot, for a time, how many people depended on him. He ended by pointing out to them that he had fixed that mistake in the second Schmeling fight and that they could fix their mistakes, too.

'Now, those guys listening to him were tough characters,' Krem said. 'He was taking an awful chance talking to them that way. But you could tell by their faces that what Joe said hit home. I'm telling you right now that Joe Louis is a great man and a great American. I went to school at Notre Dame and I knew Knute Rockne [Notre Dame's famous football coach, considered by many as the greatest in his profession]. Until I met Joe, I never met a sports figure that measured up to Knute. Joe does.' "

*Private Joe Louis cut a striking figure in his military garb. This picture was taken a week after Louis enlisted in the army.*

*(Above) Army calisthenics were surely a breeze for world heavyweight champion Louis, shown in the foreground participating in early morning exercises. (Below) Louis arrives at Fort Dix, a facility with a gymnasium where he could train for upcoming bouts.*

lines, yet desperately wanting to believe it was united against a common foe, Louis was a symbol of national unity.[83]

## Back to Basics

Louis began his career as a private even though the army had offered to commission him as an officer. Louis was well aware of his lack of formal education and did not feel he was qualified to be an officer and command other men. He wanted to remain with soldiers who had backgrounds similar to his own.

While Louis continued to train as a regular GI, higher-ups in the army had ideas about how Joe should serve. Army officials knew of Joe's fight to benefit Navy Relief and thought it would be appropriate for Joe to arrange another fight, this time for the benefit of Army Relief. After all, Joe was in the army now.

## Another War to Win

*When Joe Louis was serving in the U.S. Army, black American soldiers were asked to fight for the freedom of those overseas, while at home they did not enjoy the same freedoms that white Americans did. In* Fritz Pollard: Pioneer in Racial Advancement, *John M. Carroll addresses this issue. Pollard was one of the few blacks to play in the early National Football League.*

"In sports, the triumphs of the 'black auxiliaries' at the Berlin Olympics [in 1936] and Joe Louis's dramatic victory over the German boxer Max Schmeling in their 1938 rematch emphasized the incongruities between American ideals and practices. The facts that civil rights organizations were stronger and more numerous than a generation before, that the African-American press was more mature and vocal, and that the number of college-educated blacks had increased rapidly all contributed to a more vigorous insistence on fair treatment as the war approached. Given the disappointing results of the almost uncritical commitment to patriotism and victory by black leadership in World War I, a new generation of leaders in the early 1940s led by A. Philip Randolph demanded both victory over fascism abroad and victory over racism at home. Prejudice and discrimination against African-Americans remained entrenched both on the home front and in the military services, however, and progress was slow."

## Another Giant; Another Giant Risk

After conferring briefly with Mike Jacobs, Louis quickly agreed to risk his title again at no gain for himself. The Army Relief Fund would benefit from Louis's title defense against Abe Simon. Simon was another giant of a man, like Carnera and Baer. He stood six feet, six inches and weighed 260 pounds. The previous year, Simon had gone thirteen rounds with Louis before being knocked out.

Again the media praised Louis's patriotism and generosity. The army transferred him to Fort Dix in New Jersey where he could train in a new gymnasium. Although Louis didn't do everything every other soldier did, he still knew he was in the army. In addition to his daily roadwork and training at the gym, Private Louis was required to put in several hours of military training. Military training was not the only thing that was different from civilian life for the champ. Chappie's heart condition prevented him from making the trip east from Chicago. For the first time in his professional career, Louis would not have Chappie in his corner. Although Blackburn's absence was a disappointment for Louis, he was

*The Louis-Simon fight. In this photo taken in the sixth round, the giant Simon sinks to the canvas and loses the bout.*

encouraged by the thousands of GIs who stopped by to watch his workouts. Louis, once again, showed his generosity by buying three thousand dollars worth of tickets for the Simon fight and giving them to his fellow soldiers.

Before the March 27 fight, the U.S. undersecretary of war paid a special tribute to him, and the ring announcer, with great flourish, introduced him as "Private Joe Louis of the United States Army."

Once in the ring, Louis went to work. He downed the larger Simon in the second round, but Simon was saved by the bell at the end of the round. Then in the sixth, Louis dropped Simon for good. Although the giant struggled to regain his feet, Simon was counted out. In addition to Louis's donation, Mike Jacobs kicked in some of his share of the fight's earnings and Simon contributed some of his share of the receipts to the cause. Army Relief benefited by seventy-five thousand dollars.

During the rest of the year, Louis was in the ring just once more—a three-round exhibition with his old sparring partner George Nicholson. In exhibitions, the title is not at stake and usually no decision is recorded unless there is a knockout. For the rest of the war, through 1945, Louis would fight only exhibitions. He would fight such nondescript boxers as Big Boy Brown and Sugar Lip Anderson several times each, mainly finishing them off early in the match. Louis put on most of these exhibitions at remote army bases in the United States and throughout the world. Soldiers welcomed an American hero and thought of his visits as a touch of home.

## Entertaining the Troops

In addition to actual fights, Louis logged thousands of miles traveling from base to base to referee fights between GIs. Paul Stenko, who played in the National Football League as Paul Stenn, remembered Louis visiting March Field in California where Stenko was a member of the high-powered base football team:

It was really a big deal to us. Here was the heavyweight champion of the world on our isolated military post. He was someone we all looked up to. When he "reffed" our weekly fights between March Field boxers, hardly anyone was watching the fighters. All eyes were on Joe. We got to meet him after the bouts, and they took lots of pictures with him and the guys. He was quiet, but friendly. You could tell he was a class guy. He did a lot to increase the morale of the average soldier.[84]

Louis was often introduced at these exhibitions and camp fights as "the first American GI to knock out a Nazi," in a reference to his having beaten German Max Schmeling in 1938.

How much Louis meant as a symbol to American servicemen, especially black servicemen, is evident in a 1944 Army Signal Corps film. The film, *The Negro Soldier*, was supervised by Colonel Frank Capra, who as a civilian was one of Hollywood's leading directors. The film was designed to increase enthusiasm for the war among black servicemen, and the narrator explained the war in terms of a boxing match. Footage from Louis's fights, especially his knockout of Schmeling, was spliced into the film.

## A Big Loss

When Louis got back to camp from one of his trips, a discouraging telegram from Roxborough awaited him. Roxy informed Louis that Chappie Blackburn was hospitalized with pneumonia. Louis requested, and was granted, a five-day leave. He immediately went to Chicago and visited his beloved trainer in the hospital.

The trainer and his boxing pupil chatted about the latest fight and other bouts

*Louis worked hard to boost the morale of fellow soldiers. Here, Louis instructs boxing rookies at Fort Riley in 1942.*

during Louis's daily visits to Chappie's room. Blackburn looked older and thinner, but he appeared to be recovering.

A few days after Louis returned to his military post, he was called to the base office to receive a telegram. Like many who lived at that time, Louis knew a telegram was seldom associated with good news. Louis's fears were well founded. The telegram stated that Chappie had died. He seemed to be getting better after he left the hospital but then suffered a fatal heart attack.

The army granted Louis another furlough to attend Blackburn's funeral. The loss of Chappie was a very hard experience for Joe. He recalled, "When the dirt went down on that coffin, I knew my life would never be the same."[85]

*Louis meets Jackie Robinson, who would make a name for himself as the first modern-day black to play major league baseball.*

## Meeting Another Legend

Because of Louis's interest in horses and his experience at his Spring Hill ranch, the military assigned him to Fort Riley, Kansas, a cavalry post, after he finished basic training.

One of the first people Louis met at Fort Riley was Jackie Robinson. Robinson was still some years away from being the first modern-day black to play major league baseball, but he had a reputation as a fine all-around athlete. He was a star running back on the UCLA football team, as well as an outstanding baseball player, basketball player, and track and field athlete.

Robinson complained to Louis that he couldn't play on the Fort Riley football and baseball teams because they were segregated. Robinson was also denied a chance to become an officer when he was refused enrollment in officer candidate school.

## Going to Bat

The discrimination black servicemen were experiencing in the military bothered Louis, as well as others who felt the effects of racial intolerance. How could America say it was fighting to make all people of the world free, especially from Nazi oppression, and expect blacks to fight when blacks were victims of racism in the United States? It was a logical question. Louis reflected:

> That made me mad, real mad. I knew I had influence, I knew I was raising money for the army and the navy, so I took myself and my influence over to

Brigadier General Donald Robinson [an officer Louis had known before] and asked him about this discrimination in ball playing. He apologized. Then he said he wanted Robinson and other qualified Negroes to play on both [football and baseball] teams.[86]

From then on blacks played on all sports teams at Fort Riley and other military bases.

## Another Assist

Louis would again use his influence to help Robinson and others. Robinson was a college graduate at the time, but was turned down, like many other blacks with college educations and degrees, when he applied to officer candidate school (OCS). Louis saw the injustice of the situation and decided to do something about it. Louis remembered how the army, despite his lack of formal education, wanted to make him an officer almost automatically. Now, college-educated blacks were denied an opportunity to become officers.

Robinson remembered Louis's assistance:

> Louis responded [to the situation] by making a few phone calls—one to Truman Gibson, a special civilian assistant to the secretary of war, to inform him of the situation black recruits were facing at Ft. Riley. Gibson responded by flying out to Kansas to meet with Joe, me, and other black soldiers. Within days of the meeting, things were worked out.[87]

Robinson and eighteen other black soldiers who had been turned down were now admitted to OCS. All successfully completed the school and became U.S. Army officers.

## Family Man

While Louis was in the service, Marva told him she was going to have a baby; he was overjoyed with the news. A daughter, Jacqueline, named in honor of Chappie, whose first name was Jack, was born in February 1943 while Joe was stationed at Fort Riley. Marva decided to move to Kansas so she and Jackie, as they called the baby girl, could be closer to Joe. But Marva moved back to Chicago after a few weeks because Joe was still traveling—this time for the army. Marva finally had enough of Joe's absences and his desire to continue to box; she divorced Joe in 1945. When Joe was discharged from the service, he spent more time with Marva and Jackie; he and Marva were remarried in July 1946.

## Continuing to Fight

No matter where Louis was in the service, he did what he could to overcome racism. He was a positive and powerful force in the fight for civil rights. It would be wrong to call him a voice against discrimination, because he did not make speeches on the order of Martin Luther King Jr. or Malcolm X, but in his own way he brought about change.

As he refereed matches on military bases or fought the short-round exhibitions, he let everyone know that he would not appear if blacks and whites were i segregated seating. In London, he protested when British theaters had black and white seating sections—the barriers were then removed.

He was also offended by how black servicemen were treated while riding buses back and forth to military bases. In the South, long before the war, it wasn't uncommon for blacks to have to "ride in the back of the bus." At Fort Bragg, North Carolina, blacks couldn't even ride on just any bus. They had to ride certain buses that were "for blacks only."

Louis spoke to a friend at the Pentagon. In a short time, segregation was barred at all military bases. Louis looked back on his forty-six-month tour of duty in the military, a time when he sacrificed boxing income that could have totaled in the millions of dollars, with no regrets. Like millions of men and women who served in World War II, he felt a duty and served. He said:

> I grew up in the army. Army life changed me. It took me away from Roxy, Mr. Black, and Chappie. When I didn't have them around to think for me and tell me what to eat and when to go to bed, I had to figure things out for myself.[88]

Louis was discharged from service in October 1945. Major General Kens presented Louis with the Legion of Merit medal "for exceptionally meritorious conduct" and told how valuable Louis had been to the morale of the armed services. Louis said, simply, "It made me feel great."[89] Perhaps America's sincere admiration for Joe Louis made it easier for whites to eventually treat blacks with more respect.

Chapter

# 9 A Civilian Again

Joe Louis faced many challengers when he returned to civilian life in late 1945. He had long been inactive as a boxer—over four years had passed since his last championship fight, and he was now thirty-two years old, quite old for a professional athlete at that time. He had the financial responsibility of supporting his daughter and Marva, even though divorced. He had accumulated staggering debt by not fighting and by getting advances from Jacobs. His business ventures had failed. His confidant, Chappie Blackburn, had died.

## Back to Boxing

The first order of business for Louis was to defend his title in a true championship fight. For more than four years, he had boxed very little except to spar for the benefit of Allied troops in remote military locations. Now he needed an attractive championship match that could accomplish several things. He needed to pay back loans to Mike Jacobs and John Roxborough, who had lent him large sums while he was earning only a few dollars a month in the army. He faced a large tax obligation to the federal government. But most important, he needed to reestablish his position as the top heavyweight fighter in the world.

The opponent chosen to help Louis do all of this was Billy Conn, who was still remembered by many as the man who almost beat Louis in 1941 but lost the match when he tried to match power punches with the champ. Jacobs tried to arrange a Louis-Conn fight when both were in the military, but military officials wouldn't allow it. Now nothing stood in the way, and the fight was set for June 19, 1946. Louis would train for six months to try to get his edge back.

When Louis went to his usual training camp site in Pompton Lakes, New Jersey, he had a new man in charge of his corner, Manny Seamon. Seamon had been Joe's assistant trainer while Chappie was alive and had actually been in Joe's corner during the Abe Simon fight when Chappie was too sick to make the trip. But he was no Chappie. In Louis's mind, no one would ever be, but Seamon was still a capable boxing trainer.

The long time away from serious competition, coupled with age, had slowed Louis's reflexes and taken away some of his stamina. Louis sensed this and worked hard to get into top condition. He put an emphasis on roadwork, running up to eight or ten miles a day on the rural roads

*Chappie's death left Louis without a boxing trainer. Manny Seamon (pictured) filled the void when he became Louis's new trainer in 1946.*

around his training camp. He also worked extensively on his timing, getting to where he could throw the right punches in the amount of time he wanted. Still, despite the hard work and long hours, Louis did not look particularly sharp to some reporters, and they said so in their articles covering the preparations to the fight. There was a sense that Conn, who came so close before, had a real chance this time.

## Conn II

Forty-five thousand people arrived at Yankee Stadium on the night of June 19. Ringside seats, costing one hundred dollars, sold out quickly. So did the cheaper bleacher seats, but many others—the stadium could hold a crowd of eighty thousand—went unsold.

Many people stayed home to watch the Louis-Conn bout on television—it was the first boxing match televised in the United States. Fewer than ten thousand people owned TV sets at the time, and most of them lived along the Eastern Seaboard, with New York having the biggest share of viewers.

Conn, who used speed and courage to do so well in the first fight, planned to use the same tactics in the rematch. He would jab Louis and dance away, or so he thought.

From the opening bell, Louis bore in on Conn. Conn could dodge and move away, but he couldn't land any significant punches. His performance would not help him in the eyes of the fight judges when it came time to score the fight, provided that neither fighter scored a knockout.

Conn continued to backpedal, throwing only long lefts that had no power because he was moving away from the target. Louis couldn't do much damage either, although he was the more aggressive fighter. Conn slipped while trying to dodge Louis's punches in both the fourth and the sixth rounds. Each time he got up quickly.

Before the eighth round Louis told Seamon and the other cornermen that he was going to look for an opening and try to finish Conn. Joe got in quick jabs. Conn moved in, as if to clinch, but Louis unleashed a quick combination—right uppercut, left hook, right cross. Conn missed a punch, but clinched. When the referee separated them, instead of moving back as he had most of the night, Conn moved in. His action was a mistake. Louis recalled, "I stepped to one side, put a hard right to his jaw, and he went down and was counted

*Louis pounds on opponent Billy Conn, sending him down for the count. (Below) Louis raises his hand in victory after this highly publicized rematch with Conn.*

out."[90] Conn went flat on his back but struggled to his feet; by then referee Eddie Jacobs had already counted to ten. Louis retained his championship for the twenty-second time.

As had been the pattern throughout his career, whenever Louis lost or had a difficult time in the ring, he invariably won the rematch very convincingly. The pattern held again.

## Where the Money Went

After five years of anticipation, the rematch with Conn lacked drama. It wasn't as electrifying as the fight of 1941. Some even said it was a financial bust. Mike Jacobs, in his overstated way, predicted a three-million-dollar gate (money taken in at the fight). Instead, the gate was two million dollars. Nevertheless, the fight drew well. It was the most profitable in Louis's career and the second most profitable fight of all time at that point.

The fight earned Louis $600,000. However, most of the money was spent before it was earned. His managers got $140,000. Marva got $66,000. New York State deducted $30,000 upfront in taxes. Jacobs and Roxy collected their long-standing loans from Louis's military days—that was another $200,000. And $115,000 went to pay Louis's 1941 tax obligation. Although these payments resolved his past financial debts, Louis still

### Looking for a New Champ

*When Louis was discharged from the service in 1945 and returned to fighting, much speculation arose as to who could take his crown. No one he fought at the time was able to meet the challenge, so boxing writer Don Dunphy, in an article entitled "The Man Who Can Lick Joe Louis," offered his opinion.*

"I think we can all agree that Louis rates a place apart in ring history. You can argue how he would have measured up against the Manassa Mauler [Jack Dempsey's nickname] in his prime, or the John L. [Sullivan] who came roaring out of Massachusetts, or that Fancy Dan of the brawling art, Gentleman Jim Corbett, or any one of a dozen top heavies, but I still think that against any of them, the Joe Louis of 1937—maybe even the Joe Louis of 1947—would wind up with his mitt held high in victory.

Who, then, can do the trick? None of the top-ranking heavyweights around today seems to have what it takes. [Billy] Conn proved he wasn't the man for the job. [Tami] Mauriello did little more than give the champ a workout—not even a strenuous one at that. Judged by what they've shown to date, all the lesser lights in the beef division [heavyweights] are a long way, both physically and mentally, from a meeting with Joe.

It may be that in the next few years a Sanders Cox, a Jackie Cranford, a Billy Fox, or even a Bruce Woodcock [all boxers of the time] might develop into strong contender material. All four are comers. Handled properly, any one of them might well be the lad to take the title away from the grave gent who has held it for almost a decade."

*None of the four mentioned boxers ever became champion—by defeating Louis or anyone else—and none of them even got close to being a top challenger.*

owed more federal taxes on what he had just earned. The fighter was in the 90 percent tax bracket, and no loopholes existed before the war to reduce the burden. It was only much later in life that the government decided to "excuse" Louis's large tax liability—the government agreed not to hound Louis for the more than one million dollars he owed, but simply to tax him on future earnings from that point on. The government made this agreement with Louis for two reasons. It knew there was little chance of ever collecting fully what Louis owed, and most of his tax problems were caused when he was serving his country in World War II and donating money to war relief causes.

## "And Still Champeen"

Marva and Joe were remarried right after the Conn fight; Joe again promised to pay more attention to her and their daughter. And while things seemed more peaceful on the home front, Louis still needed to fight to get out of debt and to maintain the lifestyle he desired.

Tami Mauriello, a home-grown product of the Bronx, was Louis's next opponent on September 18, 1946. He was a stocky, barrel-chested slugger with an impressive knockout record and was also the leading contender at the time.

Mauriello, a tough brawling fighter, waded right into Louis. He even landed some good punches, sending Louis into the ring ropes. Then Mauriello miscalculated. He thought he hurt Louis, but what he hurt was the champ's pride. Louis looked composed to those seated at ringside. Mauriello bore in and got dropped to the canvas by Louis's left hook. Mauriello got up only to be sent to the canvas again by another left hook, followed by a right. It was still the first round. Referee Arthur Donovan counted the challenger out as he was draped over the middle ring rope.

For the first time in his career, Louis smiled as he walked back to his corner. Remember, one of the rules laid down for Louis by his managers was to never gloat over knocking out a white boxer. Louis, by now, was such a revered figure that his little smile offended no one.

Ring announcer Harry Balogh, himself quite a celebrity because of his distinctive and somewhat ungrammatical and unique pronunciations, bellowed into the microphone that Louis was the winner by a knockout in the first round "and still champeen."

Louis would later describe his feelings: "[It] was the last time I really felt like my old self in the ring. I had complete control, energy, power."[91] In the next three years that Louis held the title, and in his comeback attempts in 1950 and 1951, he would never look better than he did finishing Mauriello in one round.

## Life Outside the Ring

The money Louis earned in the Mauriello fight disappeared quickly. Louis continued to put more money into bad investments. He had opened the Chicken Shack restaurant in Detroit, which did well for a while, but eventually failed. The same thing happened with his nightclub in Chicago, Swingland. It too did well when it first opened, but proved to be an income drain rather than a moneymaker.

*Although touted as a tough challenger, Tami Mauriello proved to be no match for Louis. Here, Louis floors Mauriello in the opening round of their title bout.*

Louis continued, though, to get involved in outside business deals. Most required little of him financially—just the use of his famous name, but they didn't produce much income either. Among the businesses that used his name were the Joe Louis Restaurant in Harlem and the Superior Life Insurance Company, backed by prominent members of the black community. A milk company gave Louis a rather modest sum (twenty thousand dollars) to call itself the Joe Louis Milk Company.

In 1946 he fought exhibition bouts in Mexico and Hawaii. In 1947 it was more exhibitions, this time in Central and South America. Joe Louis, as the large crowds at exhibitions proved, was an international hero, but Joe and Marva and their traveling party spared no expense on the tour, and very little real income was realized.

On May 24, 1947, Joseph Louis Barrow Jr. was born. Louis, who truly loved children, was thrilled with "Little Joe's" arrival, but the pressure to provide income was even greater now than before.

## Another Title Defense

Joe Baksi, a pretty good fighter from the coal region of Pennsylvania, was a logical opponent for Louis. He had a good record, could punch, and was experienced enough to take on the champion. Despite what would have been a sizeable payday for him, Baksi refused to fight the champion in a title defense. Baksi, when prodded by Louis's managers, didn't even want to fight Louis in an exhibition. So the search for an opponent willing to step in the ring with Louis and take a shot at the heavyweight championship continued. The search turned up Jersey Joe Walcott, a boxer who was actually several months older than Louis. He did not have a very distinguished career, but his recent fights had given Walcott some standing in the boxing community. At first the fight was to be a ten-round exhibition, but the New York State Athletic Commission would not sanction the bout unless it was for the championship and fifteen rounds in length. If Walcott won, he'd be the new champion. Few thought that could happen. Louis was a heavy favorite over the man

*(Left) Outside the ring, Louis lent his name to many businesses, including the Joe Louis Restaurant in Harlem. (Above) Louis with his son, "Little Joe," who was born in 1947.*

who had once been his sparring partner. They climbed through the ropes at Madison Square Garden on December 5, 1947.

Walcott, although underrated by some writers, was a crafty veteran of the ring and hungry for the title. He hit and moved away in the first round but then held his ground and put Louis on the ring floor with a hard right. As he had with Mauriello, Louis bounced up, but he couldn't finish Walcott. In the fourth, Walcott again decked Louis, who didn't bounce up so quickly this time. Louis continued to stalk Walcott through the rest of the fight but couldn't finish him. In the late rounds, Walcott, thinking he was so far ahead on points that it didn't matter, hardly bothered to throw a punch. Still Louis couldn't score a knockout.

When the fight was over, the decision was close and one that was split—referee Ruby Goldstein had Walcott winning by a round, but both judges had Louis winning by a wider margin. Louis retained his title, but he wasn't pleased with his effort:

> I was so disgusted with myself and the way I fought that I started climbing out of the ring before the decision was announced, but my corner [his seconds] pulled me back. I didn't care about the decision. I knew I won, since

### Sound Advice

*The late tennis champion Arthur Ashe, one of the first blacks to attain a high ranking in the sport, wrote in his acclaimed memoir* Days of Grace *about the necessity of securing sound financial advice. This guidance was something that Joe Louis badly needed but didn't receive, at least not until it was too late.*

"Good lawyers and financial experts come in all colors, genders, and backgrounds. Read before signing any contracts, but then stick to the agreements you sign. Resist the urge to try to wriggle out of financial arrangements and obligations. A wise person decides slowly but abides by these decisions. Be prudent in your generosity. In fact, although charity is important, dispense with generosity if you must; deal first with your primary responsibilities.

For some athletes and entertainers, generosity is their gravest problem. Among boxers, for example, Joe Louis was legendary for his charity toward all, which he often expressed in hundred-dollar tips. At one point, Louis owed the United States government four million dollars in income tax, which the government forgave (it had no hope of ever collecting this money). If I remember correctly, Joe eked out a living near the end of his life as a greeter in a Las Vegas casino."

*Jersey Joe Walcott nearly made headway in his bid for the title when he faced Louis in the ring on December 5, 1947. Although Louis won the fight and retained his title, the match was close.*

> Walcott didn't come to me. After all, I was the champion, and he had to take the crown from me.[92]

## The Last Fight—Almost

Walcott and Louis signed for a rematch for June 23, 1948. But before that, Louis took Marva and a group of friends to England and France. He was to fight exhibitions and earn eighty thousand dollars, but the promoters (European, not Louis's) went broke and Louis got only forty thousand dollars. This amount barely covered expenses. On this trip Marva again caught Joe with another woman, and the marriage was again in trouble. Marva would divorce him, for good this time, in 1949, although she and Joe would remain on friendly terms. When Louis got back to the States, he put everything else out of his mind and concentrated on training.

Rain delays forced two postponements of the Walcott fight, which hurt the attendance. Neither Louis nor Walcott did much once the actual fight started at Yankee Stadium. Walcott continued to be overly cautious and Louis tried to take the fight to him. Once, in round five, Louis got close enough to Walcott to get knocked down by a right. But after Louis got up, the fight resumed its cat-and-mouse flavor. At one time, the referee asked the boxers to give the crowd more of a fight. Referee Frank Fullam continued

*Louis redeemed himself in his rematch against Walcott. Here, Louis unleashes a flurry of blows to bring Jersey Joe down for the count.*

to urge Walcott to mix it up with the champ. Walcott stopped dancing away, and Louis's greater power allowed him to get in some hard blows. In the eleventh, Louis forced Jersey Joe into the ropes and summoned the strength that champions always seem to find. A final flurry dropped Walcott for the count.

Once again, Louis redeemed himself in a rematch with a fighter who to some observers made him look bad.

Sensing that Louis was near, if not at, the end of a glorious boxing career, the crowd gave the longtime champion a standing ovation.

Louis announced on the radio in a postfight interview that he would not fight again. Although he no doubt meant what he said, he was not really ready to leave the ring.

## Retirement

Throughout the rest of 1948 and all of 1949 Louis fought meaningless exhibitions, not real fights. In a way he did make good on his statement to retire. Finally, he made his retirement official on March 1, 1949. Joe Louis was the first heavyweight champion to retire undefeated. (Schmeling had beaten him before he became champ.)

He had vacated his title and would become part of the process in deciding who would become the new champion.

Louis, with the help of Truman Gibson (the man who held an influential government position and helped him to help black servicemen during the war), formed the International Boxing Commission

(IBC) with Jim Norris and Arthur Wirtz. Norris owned two National Hockey League (NHL) franchises—the Chicago Blackhawks and the Detroit Red Wings. Wirtz was also very wealthy. The IBC was much like Jacobs's 20th Century Sporting Club. It controlled who fought for what title. Gibson and Louis had signed the leading contenders in the heavyweight class and sold these contracts to Norris and Wirtz. Louis would also get a yearly salary from the IBC.

After officially announcing his retirement, Louis and the IBC declared Jersey Joe Walcott and Ezzard Charles (a man who had been the light heavyweight champion but gave up his title because he felt he was ready to step up to heavyweight) the two leading contenders for Louis's open title. The NBA (National Boxing Association), which was an association of state athletic commissions, accepted this judgment and sanctioned a title fight between the contenders. Charles won this fight but lost the championship to Walcott at a later date.

Through the rest of 1949, 1950, and the first half of 1951, Louis stayed active by fighting exhibitions. These meaningless fights did nothing to help his financial situation and little to keep him in shape.

## Paying the Taxman

The Internal Revenue Service (IRS) finally conducted a thorough audit of Louis's finances for the last ten years. Louis still owed $500,000 in taxes, interest, and penalties. Much of Louis's financial failure could be attributed to his lifestyle. He always went first class and took along plenty of friends. He was also generous to family and friends, and even to strangers. When Louis was in need of sound financial advice, there was none. Neither Roxborough nor Jacobs ever tried to curb his spending. They simply lent him what he said he needed, whenever he asked for it.

While Truman Gibson, a sincere man who truly had Louis's best interests at heart, tried to get the government to accept a compromise to settle Joe's tax liability, the IRS was unwilling to negotiate. There was only one way for Joe ever to hope to get out of debt. Louis had to fight Ezzard Charles for the championship.

Because Louis and the IBC had a hand in Ezzard Charles's fighting for the vacant heavyweight title, when it came time for Louis and Charles to fight, Louis was able to secure a 35 percent share of the receipts, while Charles settled for 20 percent. These were the usual percentages, but ordinarily the champion, now Charles, would get the larger share. Although Louis was now a challenger, many, including Charles, still regarded him as the champ.

## Back to Boxing

Louis's enthusiasm for fighting had faded. He no longer had the zest for training. He cut his roadwork in half, only three miles a day. When he weighed in, he was about 10 pounds too heavy, 218. Louis had also lost much of the one thing that made him an exceptional athlete and champion—his lightning reflexes. His hands were no longer as fast, nor as strong. Pride was nearly all Louis took into the ring with him.

*Once known for his lightning speed, an exhausted Louis took a beating in the ring with the younger and quicker Ezzard Charles.*

The fight was a sad commentary on a former champion. Charles was much quicker than Louis, who hardly ever caught up to the young, new champion to inflict any damage. Charles, who won all but three rounds, dominated the fifteen-round fight. Louis was a shell of what he had been. Louis was so exhausted toward the end of the fight that he had to be lifted off of his stool by his cornermen to start the final round. Charles easily could have finished the fight with a knockout, but probably reflecting the thinking of much of the nation, he could not bring himself to humiliate Louis. He held back for the last three minutes, allowing Louis to end the fight standing up.

As sad as it was, out of financial necessity, Louis had to continue his comeback. Fighting lesser lights of the heavyweight division, Louis won eight fights in late 1950 and early 1951. In October, he faced a young contender, Rocky Marciano. Because Marciano, soon to be heavyweight

champion himself, was such a wild swinger, Louis looked good early in the fight. He actually won three of the first five rounds. But then his age, coupled with Marciano's youth, turned the tide. Marciano, a savage puncher, dropped Louis with a left. Then he put him through the ropes with a right. With Louis on the ring apron with his feet in the ring, referee Ruby Goldstein stopped the fight.

## A Saddened Dressing Room

After the fight, the mood was somber in Louis's dressing room. Sugar Ray Robinson, a great middleweight champion, wept

*Scenes from the decisive Louis-Marciano bout. (Above) Louis and Marciano hammer away at each other. (Below) Marciano sends Louis sprawling backwards into the ropes. The fight marked the end of Louis's career in the ring.*

## The Comeback Trail

*In 1950, tax obligations and other financial problems forced Joe Louis to fight again. His opponent was Ezzard Charles, and Louis was soundly beaten. In the 1940–1950 volume of* This Fabulous Century, *Time-Life Books included an excerpt from the October 9, 1950, issue of* Newsweek.

"To at least one observer, it seemed that men who sadly watched the humiliation of Joe Louis last week in Yankee Stadium were really feeling sorry for themselves. So many, in the uncomfortably long span of Louis's greatness, had themselves picked up fortyish weight and lost twentyish confidence since the first night they saw him come into Yankee Stadium. And anything they felt may have been made more acute by the fact that Louis's story began and ended on the same spot: the Stadium's garishly lighted, 20-by-20-foot patch of canvas. There in 1935 he had instantly excited them . . . [against Primo Carnera]. There, only a year later, Max Schmeling found the flaw. . . . Later Schmeling said the kid would never be able to forget [the defeat], and in a way he was right. In 1938, the German [Schmeling] was shipped from the Stadium to a hospital after just two minutes and 4 seconds of exposure to the kid's rage.

Last week, pressed for cash to settle an income-tax bill, he paid the Stadium one more visit.

For moments in the fourth and tenth rounds, Louis's left shot out with some of its remembered cobra sureness; the right followed with something of the full, overhand pitch that had rubbled so many men. But Charles turned Louis's face into a puffed, bloody lump and made him grab a ring rope in the fourteenth round to avoid falling. As a man with little experience in taking a beating, Louis took this one well, stubbornly marching into it."

*In their 1950 fight, Louis cringes as he takes a punch from Ezzard Charles.*

*Louis hovers over a beaten opponent.*

openly. Marciano paid a visit, and he was crying, too. Louis, as always, was calm and quiet. He greeted Ezzard Charles, who came to pay his respects. Louis, gracious as ever, said, "The better man won. I'm not looking for sympathy from anyone."[93]

> Marciano called it [the punch that ended the fight and Louis's career] "the saddest punch of my life. How else could I feel seeing one of the finest sportsmen that ever lived lying on the canvas?" Louis believed him. "When he defeated me," [Louis said], "I think it hurt him more than it hurt me."[94]

Thus ended what may be the greatest career in heavyweight boxing history, perhaps even the greatest career of any individual athlete. Louis compiled a record of sixty-eight wins, three losses, and no draws. He held the title from 1937 to 1949, longer than any champion of any division.

With the Korean War going on, Louis embarked on an exhibition tour of the Far East. Much as he had done in World War II, Louis performed for the benefit of Allied troops. He stopped in Japan and Formosa, and over a period of several months, staged a dozen exhibition fights. To no one's surprise, Louis won them all. Later, Louis briefly tried professional wrestling. Of course, he was the "good guy" and always triumphed over the villain.

Louis had other setbacks. In 1953 his mother, always a source of strength, and Mike Jacobs died. He seemed like a rudderless ship in a stormy sea. However, 1953 was not without its positives. Hollywood produced *The Joe Louis Story*. Coley Wallace in the title role was actually a pretty good heavyweight boxer and bore a strong resemblance to a younger Joe Louis.

Louis had formed an advertising agency with black photographer Billy Rowe, and it managed to make some money as well as to occupy Louis's time.

Around this time Louis met, and later married, Rose Morgan, a woman who owned a large beautician business in Harlem. The marriage worked for a while, but in 1957, two years after the wedding, Louis and Rose separated, and the marriage was annulled.

In 1959 Louis married another woman who could afford to give him a decent lifestyle, Martha Malone Jefferson. She was the first black female attorney admitted to the practice of law in California. Martha's income gave Louis the time and the resources to pursue his longtime passion for golf. Though not a great golfer, he was well above average for an amateur his age. He often shot in the seventies in various celebrity and charity tournaments.

In the 1960s, Louis became addicted to cocaine. The moment marked the beginning of the end of this once-proud, beloved champion.

*Chapter*

# 10 Requiem for a Heavyweight

The chapter title is borrowed from a critically acclaimed TV drama of the 1950s. Though not related to Joe Louis, the play's title is appropriate. Hardly an American alive at the time was not moved by his death. Those who knew him best were eloquent in their praise. The Reverend Jesse L. Jackson seemed to find the right words:

> This is not a funeral, this is a celebration. Often we tred on godlike descriptions as we describe our relationship with Joe. With Joe Louis we had made it from the guttermost to the uttermost; from slaveship to championship. Usually the champion rides on the shoulders of the nation and its people, but in this case, the nation rode on the shoulders of the hero, Joe. When Joe fought Max Schmeling, what was at stake was the confidence of a nation with a battered ego and in search of resurrection, and the esteem of a race of people.
>
> Joe made the lion lie down with the lamb. The black, brown, and white—the rich and the poor were together, and none were afraid. God sent Joe from the black race to represent the human race. He was the answer to the sincere prayers of the disinherited and dispossessed. Joe made everybody somebody.
>
> We all feel bigger today because Joe came this way. He was in the slum, but the slum wasn't in him. Ghetto boy to man, Alabama sharecropper to champion. Let's give Joe a big hand clap. This is a celebration. Let's hear it for the champ. Let's hear it for the champ![95]

It was entirely appropriate that Rev. Jackson had so large a part in Joe Louis's final service. When he was born in 1941, he was named for the heavyweight champion of the world. His full name is Jesse Louis Jackson.

## Always a Hero

Joe Louis's last years were not pleasant for him, nor for the millions who still regarded him as a hero. He had problems with drugs and alcohol. He worked as a "greeter" in a Las Vegas casino. He allowed himself to be exploited by those who only wanted to capitalize on his name. He had bouts with mental illness, suffered a disabling stroke and encountered other setbacks. But one thing never waivered. Joe Louis was until his death, and still is today, a true American hero.

*Outside the ring, life for the aging Louis was difficult. The ex-fighter battled mental illness for years, during which time he worked as a greeter in a Las Vegas casino.*

As he continued to use cocaine, Louis's life appeared to bottom out in June 1969. He was rushed to a New York hospital after collapsing from severe pain. Apparently, there was more than just drug abuse involved. Louis had become very paranoid.

> He would not eat food that Martha [his wife] had not prepared, fearing some unknown poisoner. Martha had to travel with him, packing a hotplate and canned soups so she could cook for Louis in their hotel room. His most persistent fear was that the Mafia was trying to gas him. He taped over air-conditioning and heating ducts, and smeared mayonnaise on cracks in the ceiling in a futile attempt to block the gas. He thought strangers were following him. He had trouble sleeping, and when he did sleep, he kept his clothes on and piled pillows and furniture around the bed, forming a makeshift cave to protect himself against his own imagination.[96]

## Fighting with Demons

Several doctors were not able to convince Louis that the demons haunting him were in his own mind. His well-intentioned family tried to have Joe committed to a Colorado mental institution, but he thwarted their plans and actually made a call to

President Richard M. Nixon. Louis didn't get through to Nixon but did reach an aide. Because of the publicity surrounding the family's attempt to commit him and the would-be presidential phone call, the media became aware of the situation. When the news of Louis's mental problems became public, the general response was somewhat vague and mostly sympathetic.

Eventually, Louis was hospitalized and made some progress in overcoming his illness. He was released, and an old friend hired Louis to meet and greet guests in a Las Vegas casino.

For a while the former champion returned to the clinic regularly as an outpatient. Joe stopped going back to Colorado for treatment eventually, but the fact that he held his job as a greeter at Caesar's Palace hid the true nature of his illness. He seemed gentle, genial, humble, and friendly—just the way most people remembered him or expected him to be. Louis would continue this job well into the seventies.

In October 1977, at the age of sixty-three, Louis suffered a severe heart attack. While he was in the hospital, Louis suffered a cerebral hemorrhage (a stroke). Louis was discharged from the hospital in a wheelchair and had difficulty speaking, and would remain wheelchair bound and

### Job Description for a Boxer

*Joe Louis and others who boxed for a living were special young men. They were talented, especially the successful ones, but they were also hard-working people. Thomas Hauser talks about what it takes to be a professional fighter in his book* Black Lights: Inside the World of Professional Boxing.

"Boxing is one of the few professions that give people from the underclass an opportunity to earn large sums of money and be heroes in their native land. It offers a young man hope, and the possibility that he will someday possess a world title once held by a god like Joe Louis or Sugar Ray Robinson. There is a unique importance to the heroes of old because they stand for the proposition that greatness in boxing is not a mirage. But in reality most fighters never become champions. The vast majority never even advance to the status of 'main event' fighters. And along the way a price is paid—by some, for good value in return; for others, not so good. The price is high.

Being a fighter is more than a job; it's a way of life. Everything a fighter does affects his profession—What he eats, what he drinks, how he sleeps, what he does at night. Yet unless a fighter is considered a valuable 'prospect,' there's no one to push and prod him on. Thus the trade requires extraordinary self-motivation."

have speech difficulties for the rest of his life. He still held on to his job, though, as a casino greeter.

On Saturday, April 11, 1981, Louis attended a heavyweight championship fight between Larry Holmes and Trevor Berbick at Caesar's Palace. Louis was in a wheelchair, of course, and being pushed by friends. Some in the crowd recognized the ex-champ and began applauding him. Before he got to his place, the entire crowd was on its feet and applauding. It would be the champ's last standing ovation. The next morning he died at his home of a massive heart attack. Thousands paid final tribute to Louis as his body was viewed, appropriately surrounded by a military honor guard. Burial, with full military honors, was at Arlington National Cemetery.

## A Calling

Famous New York columnist Jimmy Cannon summed up Louis's contribution to boxing this way:

> It was Louis himself who acted as though prizefighting was a sacred calling and not the ugly graft [corruption] that it was. Not once in the time Joe was champion did he abuse his office. In all fights I saw him make I can't recall him striking a foul blow. There were times when Joe could have used illegal tactics without any criticism. They tried everything against him, but it never agitated him out of his stately and always honorable fury. Max Baer hit him after the bell and this would have provoked the average fighter into retaliation. But Joe looked at Baer with disgust and shambled back to his corner, the contemptuous glance the only indication that he knew he had been fouled. He made Baer quit that night and I suppose that is the classic revenge.[97]

Cannon further places Louis in historical perspective:

> There are those who will tell you that Louis was an ordinary heavyweight [but not many] who was erroneously accused of greatness because of the ineptness of his opposition. But you don't believe them. There were few as good in any age and that goes for all of them. You can start with John L. Sullivan and come right down to Jim Braddock, the one before Louis. There never was a heavyweight champion who took the chances Louis did. They were all alike to him and he fought them all. He never ducked anyone.[98]

## Dignity

Red Smith was probably the most-read sports columnist of his day. He authored the prestigious "Sports of the Times" column in the *New York Times*.

Smith wrote of Louis's impressive dignity:

> Joe Louis Barrow lived a month less than sixty-seven years. He was heavyweight champion of the world in an era when the heavyweight champion was, in the view of many, the greatest man in the world. Not once in sixty-six years was he known to utter a word of complaint or bitterness or offer an excuse for anything. To be sure, he had

nothing to make excuses about. In 71 recorded fights he lost three times.

Joe had just celebrated his twenty-first birthday when he came to New York for the first time. This was 1935, not a long time ago, yet some people still saw any black man as the stereotype darky, who loved dancing and watermelon. Some news photographer bought a watermelon and asked Joe to pose eating a slice. He refused, saying he didn't like watermelon. "And the funny thing is," said Harry Markson [a writer] telling the story, "Joe loves watermelon."

At twenty-one, this unlettered son of Alabama sharecroppers had the perception to realize what the pictures would imply and the quiet dignity to have no part in the charade. Dignity was always a word that applied to him. Dignity and candor.[99]

## A Final Footnote

In June 1993, the U.S. Postal Service paid yet another tribute to Joe Louis and his accomplishments. It issued a Joe Louis postage stamp featuring Louis in a classic boxing pose. In so doing, the USPS placed Louis in the company of presidents, statesmen, and other distinguished Americans. Joe should feel right at home.

# Notes

### Chapter 1: Down Yonder

1. Joe Louis, with Meyer Berger and Barney Nagler, "My Story," *Life*, November 8 and 15, 1948, p. 128.
2. Louis, "My Story," p. 129.
3. Louis, "My Story," p. 127.
4. Joe Louis, with Edna and Art Rust Jr., *Joe Louis: My Life*. New York: Harcourt Brace Jovanovich, 1978, p. 15.
5. Louis, *Joe Louis: My Life*, p. 16.
6. Louis, "My Story," p. 132.
7. Louis, "My Story," p. 134.
8. Louis, *Joe Louis: My Life*, p. 32.
9. Louis, *Joe Louis: My Life*, p. 33.

### Chapter 2: Joe Louis, Pro Boxer

10. Louis, *Joe Louis: My Life*, p. 34.
11. Louis, *Joe Louis: My Life*, p. 36.
12. Louis, "My Story," p. 138.
13. Louis, "My Story," p. 138.
14. Louis, *Joe Louis: My Life*, p. 44.
15. Louis, *Joe Louis: My Life*, p. 44.
16. Louis, "My Story," p. 141.
17. Chris Mead, *Champion: Joe Louis, Black Hero in White America*. New York: Charles Scribner's Sons, 1985, p. 51.
18. Louis, "My Story," p. 142.
19. Louis, "My Story," p. 142.

### Chapter 3: The Big Apple

20. Louis, "My Story," p. 148.
21. Quoted in Mead, *Champion*, p. 59.
22. Louis, *Joe Louis: My Life*, p. 60.
23. Louis, *Joe Louis: My Life*, p. 60.
24. Louis, "My Story," p. 151.
25. Quoted in Mead, *Champion*, p. 70.
26. Quoted in Mead, *Champion*, p. 71.
27. Louis, "My Story," p. 151.
28. Louis, "My Story," p. 151.
29. Quoted in Louis, "My Story," p. 151.
30. George L. Lee, *Black American Sports Heroes*. New York: Ballantine Books, 1993, p. 36.
31. Louis, "My Story," p. 151.

### Chapter 4: The First Schmeling Fight

32. Louis, *Joe Louis: My Life*, p. 80.
33. Louis, *Joe Louis: My Life*, p. 82.
34. Bob Broeg, *Don't Bring That Up*. New York: A. S. Barnes, 1946, p. 184.
35. Louis, *Joe Louis: My Life*, p. 86.
36. Louis, *Joe Louis: My Life*, p. 87.
37. Louis, *Joe Louis: My Life*, p. 87.
38. Louis, *Joe Louis: My Life*, p. 89.
39. *New York Times*, June 21, 1936, p. 11.
40. Robert Creamer, *Baseball in 1941*. New York: Viking, 1991, p. 196.
41. Duff Hart-Davis, *Hitler's Games: The 1936 Olympics*. New York: Harper & Row, 1986, p. 123.
42. Lee, *Black American Sports Heroes*, p. 39.
43. Quoted in Mead, *Champion*, p. 98.
44. Louis, *Joe Louis: My Life*, p. 91.
45. Stanley Grosshandler, personal interview, 1995.

### Chapter 5: Joe Louis, World Champion

46. Joe Louis, "My Story," p. 129.
47. Louis, "My Story," p. 130.
48. Quoted in Mead, *Champion*, p. 122.
49. Quoted in Mead, *Champion*, p. 123.
50. Louis, *Joe Louis: My Life*, p. 118.
51. Louis, *Joe Louis: My Life*, p. 119.
52. Louis, "My Story," p. 130.

### *Chapter 6: Schmeling—Rematch and Retribution*

53. Louis, "My Story," p. 133.
54. Louis, "My Story," p. 133.
55. Jack Sher, "Brown Bomber, the Story of the Champ," *Sport*, June 1946, p. 68.
56. Quoted in Mead, *Champion*, p. 139.
57. Quoted in Mead, *Champion*, p. 139.
58. Louis, "My Story," p. 133.
59. Art Donovan Jr., with Bob Drury, *Fatso*. New York: William Morrow, 1987, p. 82.
60. Sher, "Brown Bomber," p. 68.
61. Quoted in Louis, "My Story," p. 133.
62. Louis, "My Story," p. 134.
63. Russell Baker, *Growing Up*. New York: Congdon & Weed, 1982, p. 205.
64. Baker, *Growing Up*, p. 205.
65. Quoted in Mead, *Champion*, p. 157.
66. Quoted in Hart-Davis, *Hitler's Games*, p. 123.
67. Quoted in Hart-Davis, *Hitler's Games*, p. 124.
68. Louis, "My Story," p. 134.

### *Chapter 7: Taking On All Comers*

69. Louis, *Joe Louis: My Life*, p. 154.
70. Louis, *Joe Louis: My Life*, p. 154.
71. Sher, "Brown Bomber," p. 68.
72. Sher, "Brown Bomber," p. 68.
73. Quoted in Louis, *Joe Louis: My Life*, p. 167.
74. Louis, *Joe Louis: My Life*, p. 167.
75. Louis, *Joe Louis: My Life*, p. 165.
76. Mead, *Champion*, p. 211.

### *Chapter 8: Private Joe Louis, U.S. Army*

77. Mead, *Champion*, p. 209.
78. Mead, *Champion*, p. 211.
79. Louis, *Joe Louis: My Life*, p. 171.
80. Quoted in Mead, *Champion*, p. 212.
81. Quoted in Mead, *Champion*, p. 216.
82. Louis, *Joe Louis: My Life*, p. 174.
83. Mead, *Champion*, p. 214.
84. Paul Stenko (Stenn), personal interview, 1995.
85. Louis, *Joe Louis: My Life*, p. 176.
86. Louis, *Joe Louis: My Life*, p. 177.
87. Quoted in David Falkner, *Great Time Coming: The Life of Jackie Robinson*. New York: Simon & Schuster, 1995, p. 69.
88. Louis, "My Story," p. 142.
89. Louis, *Joe Louis: My Life*, p. 190.

### *Chapter 9: A Civilian Again*

90. Louis, "My Story," p. 142.
91. Quoted in Mead, *Champion*, p. 245.
92. Louis, *Joe Louis: My Life*, p. 203.
93. Quoted in Mead, *Champion*, p. 259.
94. Marc Pachter, *Champions of American Sport*. New York: Harry N. Abrams, 1981, p. 89.

### *Chapter 10: Requiem for a Heavyweight*

95. Quoted in Mead, *Champion*, p. 296.
96. Mead, *Champion*, p. 284.
97. Jimmy Cannon, *Esquire's Great Men and Moments in Sports*. New York: Harper & Brothers, 1962, p. 14.
98. Cannon, *Esquire's Great Men*, p. 18.
99. Walter "Red" Smith, *To Absent Friends from Red Smith*. New York: Atheneum, 1983, p. 172.

# For Further Reading

Dave Anderson, *In the Corner.* New York: William Morrow, 1991. A compilation of anecdotes—some amusing, others very dramatic—about what goes on behind the scenes in boxing, as well as actual fights, as seen through the eyes of some of boxing's most famous trainers. Anderson, a leading columnist for the *New York Times,* draws on a wealth of experience covering high-profile sports events to piece together this information in a revealing "insider" book about boxing. A great look at what goes into the making of a contender or champion.

Gerald Astor, "*. . . And a Credit to His Race": The Hard Life and Times of Joseph Louis Barrow, a.k.a. Joe Louis.* New York: E.P. Dutton, 1974. The title is borrowed from a tag line that was attached to any Joe Louis introduction, so much so that it became a cliche. The book develops various themes that show Louis was truly a credit to his race—the human race. It recounts Louis's historic career, gives a real feel for what Louis had to overcome to be a legendary champion, and portrays what America was like at the time Louis was champion and idol to millions.

Thomas Hauser, *The Black Lights: Inside the World of Professional Boxing.* New York: McGraw-Hill, 1986. Although the book deals with a champion, Billy Costello, who fought long after Joe Louis's career, the three-month documentation of Costello's preparation and training give great insight into the "fight game." The book takes readers into places that the general public usually never gets the opportunity to visit. Hauser, an attorney as well as an author, spent hundreds of hours with the fighter and his handlers and saw much of boxing's inner workings firsthand.

Robert Jakoubek, *Joe Louis.* New York: Chelsea House Publications, 1989. The book, from the *Black Americans of Achievement* series, features a thoughtful and meaningful introduction by Martin Luther King Jr.'s widow, Coretta Scott King. Jakoubek explores the achievements of Louis as an athlete and as a symbol of his race, both to blacks and whites. It places Louis in the context of his times.

Robert Lipsyte, *Joe Louis: A Champ for All America.* New York: Harper Collins, 1987. Lipsyte, long regarded as an outstanding sportswriter, has authored a fine biography of the Brown Bomber that is aimed at young readers. Informative but easy to read, this book is a contemporary look at a legendary champion and American hero. The book is a great way for a young reader to learn about Louis's climb to the pinnacle of his profession and his achievement of a place in American history that has been attained by a relative few. The book contains many illustrations.

Barney Nagler, *Brown Bomber: the Pilgrimage of Joe Louis*. New York: World, 1972. Nagler, a knowledgeable sportswriter, was one of two men (Meyer Berger was the other) who collaborated with Louis on a lengthy, two-part autobiographical article in *Life* magazine in 1948. In this book, Nagler devotes a significant amount of space to Louis's later life. He carefully describes how Louis's mental illness developed and its effects on his postboxing years.

Joyce Carol Oates, *On Boxing*. New York: Dolphin/Doubleday, 1987. Considered one of America's outstanding writers, Oates presents a varied glimpse into the many facets of boxing. Although it doesn't deal specifically with Joe Louis, this brief volume can enhance the reader's knowledge of boxing. Dramatic black-and-white photographs enhance the text.

# Works Consulted


**Books**

Maya Angelou, *I Know Why the Caged Bird Sings.* New York: Random House, 1969. In her widely acclaimed book dealing with growing up in depression-era rural Arkansas, the poet-author describes, among many things, what Joe Louis meant to the black community.

Arthur J. Ashe Jr., *Days of Grace: A Memoir.* New York: Alfred A. Knopf, 1993. Ashe's moving autobiography, written with Arnold Rampersad, gives great insight into what it was like to be a black athlete in the United States in a sport dominated by white players. The book contains many parallels between Ashe's struggle to get to the top of tennis and Joe Louis's rise to fame and glory as a boxer.

———, *A Hard Road to Glory: A History of the African-American Athlete, 1919–1945.* New York: Warner Books, 1988. The second volume of the three-volume set of meticulously researched books that cover all major sports in America. The section on boxing places the individual fighters—Louis, of course, among them—in perspective with the environment of their times. Explored in particular is Joe Louis's legacy.

Joe Louis Barrow Jr. and Barbara Munder, *Joe Louis: Fifty Years an American Legend.* Boston: G.D. Hall, 1990. The son of the champion takes a fond look at his father and describes how he grew up as the son of a legend.

Jimmy Cannon, *Esquire's Great Men and Moments in Sports.* New York: Harper & Brothers, 1962. In the article "Joe Louis: Greatest of Champions," included in this anthology, Cannon describes much of what made Louis great. The book contains informative and interesting articles on other sports figures.

John M. Carroll, *Fritz Pollard: Pioneer in Racial Advancement.* Urbana: Illinois University Press, 1992. History professor Carroll gives a detailed account of black football pioneer Pollard. Pollard, who named a black football team he owned after Louis—the Brown Bombers—puts Louis's career into perspective as well as what it was like to battle for civil rights much of his life.

Jack Clary, *Great Teams, Great Years—Cleveland Browns.* New York: Macmillan, 1973. Clary, a meticulous pro football historian, depicts the fabled history of this football team, including how the popularity of Joe Louis influenced the naming of the Browns.

David Falkner, *Great Time Coming: The Life of Jackie Robinson.* New York: Simon & Schuster, 1995. In this book, Falkner uses Robinson's words to tell of Robinson's struggle to become the first modern-day black major league baseball player and how Louis assisted him in the days before his professional baseball career.

Nat Fleischer and Sam Andre, *A Pictorial History of Boxing.* New York: Citadel

Press, 1959. Although lavishly illustrated with photographs, etchings, drawings, and other items, the good writing of these two editors of *Ring* magazine complements the visual aspects of the book. They cover the sport from its beginnings to the time of publication, and the book contains many dramatic action shots of Louis at the peak of his career.

Duff Hart-Davis, *Hitler's Games: The 1936 Olympics*. New York: Harper & Row, 1986. Hart-Davis's book gives great insight into the Nazi propaganda machine, especially how it exploited Max Schmeling's boxing career in conjunction with the 1936 Olympics held in Berlin.

Martin Luther King Jr., *Why We Can't Wait*. New York: Harper & Row, 1964. In his inspirational book, King cites a poignant example of Louis's standing as a symbol of hope to blacks. Many aspects of the civil rights movement of the 1960s are also included.

Joe Louis, with Edna and Art Rust Jr., *Joe Louis: My Life*. New York: Harcourt Brace Jovanovich, 1978. In his own words, Joe Louis gives a detailed description of his life. He does not gloss over his faults, nor does he dwell unduly on his accomplishments. Like the man, the book is honest and straightforward.

Chris Mead, *Champion: Joe Louis, Black Hero in White America*. New York: Charles Scribner's Sons, 1985. This is perhaps the most objective and factual of all Joe Louis biographies or autobiographies. The author does not attempt to paint Louis as a perfect hero. Mead's fair and unbiased look at the champion presents the good, the bad, and the ugly. It also gives an accurate picture of America in general, and boxing, in particular, in Louis's time. In compiling the book, Mead consulted many and varied sources for material. The book includes black-and-white photographs, several unpublished for decades.

Larry Merchant, *Ringside at the Circus*. New York: Holt, Rinehart, and Winston, 1976. Merchant, a highly regarded writer and boxing television commentator, writes of a wide variety of sports. His considerable writing on boxing in this book is particularly insightful. Much of what is included originally appeared in his thought-provoking *New York Post* columns.

James A. Michener, *Sports in America*. New York: Random House, 1976. The famed author of many best-sellers offers many opinions on American sport. His work includes a sincere tribute to Joe Louis as an athlete and citizen.

Marc Pachter, *Champions of American Sport*. New York: Harry N. Abrams, 1981. This profusely illustrated book is a companion piece to a nationwide tour of sports art. It includes an illustration of Louis and a written tribute to the champion. Many other prominent athletes are included in the book.

Jerry T. Sammons, *Beyond the Ring: The Role of Boxing in American Society*. Chicago: University of Illinois Press, 1990.

Sammons's provocative work explores the history of the relationship between American values and the sport of boxing. It highlights the importance of boxing champions throughout the years with a considerable focus on Joe Louis.

Walter "Red" Smith, *To Absent Friends from Red Smith.* New York: Atheneum, 1983. Smith, regarded by many as the greatest sportswriter of his time, covers a wide range of sports in this book. His treatment of Joe Louis may be the best article in this good collection.

Donald Spivery, ed., *Sports in America: New Historical Perspectives.* Westport, CT: Greenwood Press, 1985. This scholarly volume traces the history of sport in America from colonial times to the present. It follows sport as a major force throughout the world and its development into a multibillion-dollar business enterprise of immense proportions throughout America. Especially informative is Frederic Cople Jaher's work on Jack Johnson, Joe Louis, and Muhammad Ali.

*This Fabulous Century: 1940–1950.* New York: Time-Life Books, 1969. This series, which documents the twentieth century in words and pictures, is divided into decades. The importance of Joe Louis is evident in the edition that covers 1940–1950.

Joseph J. Vecchione, ed., *The New York Times Book of Sports Legends.* New York: Times Books, 1991. Includes the very best sports columns of the *New York Times,* as well as lengthy essays by top-flight *Times* sportswriters. Featured are the Red Smith and James P. Dawson columns on Louis and Deane McGowen's fine introductory essay.

George Vecsey, ed., *The Way It Was: Great Sports Events from the Past.* New York: McGraw-Hill, 1974. This book is a companion piece to the critically acclaimed television series *The Way It Was.* Using still photographs taken from actual motion picture footage, the book illustrates the first Joe Louis–Billy Conn fight. The text includes interviews with Louis and Conn at the time of the fight (1941) and at the time of the TV series (1974).

**Periodicals**

Caswell Adams, "Introducing the New Joe Louis," *Saturday Evening Post,* May 10, 1941.

Edward Brown, "Joe Louis, the Champion," *Life,* September 29, 1941.

Arthur Daly, "And in This Corner, Father Time," *New York Times Magazine,* June 6, 1948.

Don Dunphy, "Can It Happen to Joe Louis?" *Sport,* December 1947.

———, "Can It Happen to Joe Walcott?" *Sport,* June 1948.

———, "The Man Who Can Lick Joe Louis," *Sport,* December 1947.

———, "Open Letter to Joe Louis," *Sport,* June 1947.

Nat Fleischer, "Again, Joe Louis vs. the Field," *Sport*, March 1950.

Paul Gallico, "Citizen Barrow," *Reader's Digest*, June 1942.

Gerard Garrett, "Why Joe Louis Can't Retire," *Sport*, March 1948.

E. G. Graves, "Three Examples of Leadership," *Black Enterprise*, July 7, 1981.

Chester Higgins, "Joe Louis, Black Atlas," *Ebony*, May 1970.

John Lardner, "The New Joe Louis," *Newsweek*, June 21, 1948.

Joe Louis, with Meyer Berger and Barney Nagler, "My Story," *Life*, November 8 and 15, 1948.

Dan Parker, "Backstage at the Heavyweight Merry-Go-Round," *Sport*, September 1947.

Grantland Rice, "See Here, Joe Louis," *Sport*, June 1948.

Jack Sher, "Brown Bomber, the Story of the Champ," *Sport*, September 1946.

———, "Joe Louis Revisited," *Sport*, June 1949.

Gay Talese, "The King as a Middle-Aged Man," *Esquire*, June 1962.

*Time*, "The Money Ain't Everything," March 3, 1947.

Gene Tunney, "Was Joe Louis the Greatest?" *Colliers*, January 14, 1950.

# Index

# Credits

***Photos***

Cover photo: FPG, International

AP/Wide World Photos, Inc., 11, 18, 19, 20, 29, 41, 42, 50, 53, 58, 71, 74, 82, 84, 86 (both), 88, 89, 94, 95 (top), 98, 99 (bottom), 101, 105 (top), 107

Archive Photos, 39, 48, 49, 59, 77, 106

Library of Congress, 15, 17, 36

UPI/Corbis-Bettmann, 13, 14, 21, 22, 25, 26, 27, 32, 34, 37, 46, 54, 61, 64, 66, 67, 68, 72, 76, 78, 85, 90, 95 (bottom), 99 (top), 102, 104, 105 (bottom), 110

***Text***

Quotations from *Champion: Joe Louis, Black Hero in White America* by Chris Mead, copyright © 1985 by Chris Mead, are reprinted by permission of Scribner, a division of Simon & Schuster.

Quotations from *Joe Louis: My Life* by Joe Louis, copyright © 1978 by Jeffrey Hoffman, are reprinted by permission of Harcourt Brace & Company.

# About the Author

Jim Campbell, a freelance writer and native of Pennsylvania, is a graduate of Susquehanna University and currently the director of athletic development at Bucknell University in Lewisburg, Pennsylvania.

Sports have been important to Campbell for much of his life. In high school and college, he participated in football, basketball, baseball, and track and field. He even had a boxing career that lasted almost a full round. His employment career includes positions with the Pittsburgh Steelers, the Pro Football Hall of Fame, NFL Properties, the NFL Alumni, and the Little League Baseball Museum.

He writes a weekly column for *Pro Football Weekly* and authors several magazine articles a year. His *Golden Years of Pro Football* is now in its second printing.

He and his wife, Brenda, reside in Selinsgrove, Pennsylvania.

BLUEGRASS MIDDLE SCHOOL
MEDIA CENTER